Praise for *Here in Berlin*

Long-listed for the Andrew Carnegie Medal for Excellence
1 of the 10 Best Books of 2017 (BBC Culture)
The New York Times Book Review Editors' Choice
An ALA Notable Book

"García's new novel is ingeniously structured, veering from poignant to shocking . . . *Here in Berlin* has echoes of W. G. Sebald, but its vivid, surprising images of wartime Berlin are García's own."
—BBC Culture, 1 of the 10 Best Books of 2017

"*Here in Berlin* is a bold, innovative novel. García gives each speaker just enough space to illuminate lives and choices that might seem shocking in the present, but however uncomfortable they may be, she proves that these stories of war and belief and the failure of moral clarity are ultimately too important for the reader to look away."
—*The Dallas Morning News*

"This exquisite book brings to life the worlds of a number of characters living in Berlin. García is a talented writer, and she delivers a thought-provoking and immersive portrait of the city." —*Bustle*

"A vivid portrait of a city in flux, *Here in Berlin* follows an unnamed visitor as she encounters a host of characters, from a young Cuban POW and the son of a Berlin zookeeper to a Jewish scholar who hid in a sarcophagus for 37 days." —*PureWow*

"The stories that comprise *Here in Berlin* are beautifully related with a perfectly pitched sense of melancholy and pathos, bound into a delicate yet powerful whole by The Visitor's own struggles to preserve and renew her sense of self while forming a new perspective to live by . . . García successfully projects this truth by grounding extraordinary stories within the fabric of the everyday, while also defamiliarizing territory we presume to know well."

—*Chicago Review of Books*

"A compulsively readable, kaleidoscopic novel depicting a multicultural Berlin in the shadow of World War II, transformed by history as well as newcomers from Cuba, Angola, and Russia."

—*The National Book Review*

"*Here in Berlin* is an impeccable linguistic exercise in narratology and a brilliant exploration of the various identities we adhere to in metropolitan environments. García successfully rehumanizes a German postwar trauma of a populace that for so long coped with the making anonymous of people through genocide, the deadening speed of its capitalist structures, and the oppressive world of East Berlin. As for her readers, García adeptly passes them the torch, giving them a little nook in which they can sit and watch the characters go about their lives, spectating and writing, in the intransitive, the city of Berlin." —*Los Angeles Review of Books*

"Rich and intriguing . . . García builds a stunning landscape that's unquestionably her trademark: a layered conversation that necessarily includes the Americas about how national identity, culture, and history are shaped by communal struggle and unsettled by political circumstance . . . *Here in Berlin* is García's most striking and profound novel to date, about the need to reconcile with the past's demons to understand our present." —*NBC News Latino*

"A strong achievement of diversity—the gradual painting of a mural with many masterful brush strokes, and an expert parroting whose characters' egotism, recriminations, and melancholy all feel authentic." —*Literal*

"The novel is a tapestry of stories, a museum's worth of stories, of witness bearers, men and women who have lived through a particular moment in history, and have come out on the other side with a mouth full of narrative . . . *Here in Berlin* is unflinching in its gaze, introducing us to characters with pasts that might otherwise be buried . . . Though not considered a historical novelist, generally speaking, García's work often finds itself playing in the sandbox of history, seeking shapes and patterns in the swirls of it. *Here in Berlin*, I would argue, could be the most important book of 2017, a year that asked so many questions. The answers, we find, are sometimes behind us." —*The Miami Rail*

"A quilt of a novel that creates a hypnotic portrait of the former East German city during and after World War II . . . A poetic pastiche of rationalizations and regrets, and a testament to the challenge of reconciling a difficult past." —*BookPage*

"A well-written book on people, war, and mystery, each encounter the unnamed visitor, and the reader, has is wonderfully human: equally gritty, hard to bear, joyful, and fascinating." —*BookTrib*

"A brilliant novel, by turns hilarious and haunting, gorgeous and brutal, entertaining and profound. Cristina García masterfully weaves an intricate web of history and passion, finely tuned to the subtle music of the soul. *Here in Berlin* demonstrates exactly why García has so long been an international treasure, one who never ceases to astonish." —CAROLINA DE ROBERTIS, author of *Perla* and *The Gods of Tango*

"*Here in Berlin* is a dream visit to that City you know. To visit this City is to be filled with dark surprise and illuminated insight. It is to be infused with tragic wonder and relentless hope. Will you get home safely? You will. But you will never be the same. And that is the power of this novel by master storyteller, Cristina García. Visitor? No Longer." —DENISE CHÁVEZ, author of *The King and Queen of Comezón*

"*Here in Berlin* is a haunting portrait of place told through the shifting, kaleidoscopic stories of its people. History's long and mournful shadow follows us into contemporary lives full of secrets, regrets, and proud enduring. By the end, we are all sifting through the rubble of the twentieth century to find shards of our own buried past." —ANA MENENDEZ, author of *In Cuba I Was a German Shepherd*

"A book about endings and new beginnings, of how the past affects our present, the long shadows still cast by the Second World War, and how stories enrich the world and make up a city where the personal and the political are revealed in all their great complexities. García has written a symphony to what has passed away and to what remains and endures." —MICHELINE AHARONIAN MARCOM, author of *A Brief History of Yes*

"This novel touches on complex themes such as exile, memory, and life in wartime." —*Library Journal*

HERE IN
HERE IN
BERLIN

HERE IN

BERLIN

A NOVEL

CRISTINA GARCÍA

Counterpoint
Berkeley, California

Here in Berlin

Copyright © 2017 by Cristina García
First hardcover edition: 2017
First paperback edition: 2018

Photographs on pages 56, 101, 124, and 170 are courtesy of the author.

The Library of Congress has cataloged the hardcover edition as follows:
Names: García, Cristina, 1958– author.
Title: Here in Berlin : a novel / Christina Garcia.
Description: Berkeley, CA : Counterpoint Press, [2017]
Identifiers: LCCN 2017015332 | ISBN 9781619029590 (hardcover)
Subjects: LCSH: City and town life—Germany—Berlin—Fiction. | Berlin
   (Germany)—Fiction.
Classification: LCC PS3557.A66 H47 2017 | DDC 813/.54—dc23
LC record available at https://lccn.loc.gov/2017015332

Paperback ISBN: 978-1-64009-108-5

Cover design by Donna Cheng
Book design by Neuwirth and Associates, Inc.

Counterpoint
2560 Ninth Street, Suite 318
Berkeley, CA 94710
www.counterpointpress.com

Printed in the United States of America
Distributed by Publishers Group West, a division of Ingram
Publisher Services

10 9 8 7 6 5 4 3 2 1

For Alfredo Franco

Everyone who falls has wings . . .

—INGEBORG BACHMANN

CONTENTS

HERE IN
BERLIN

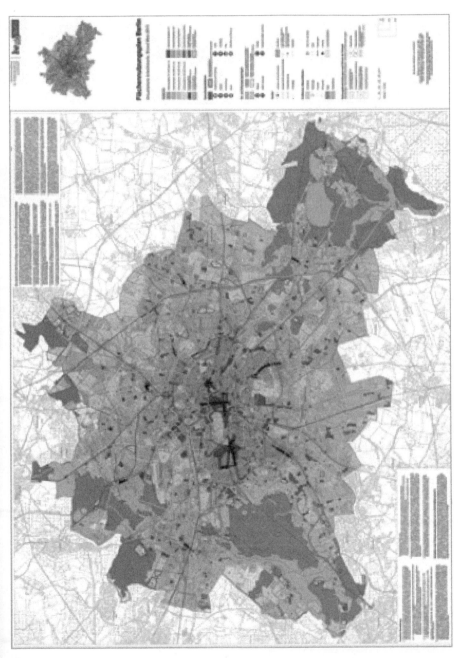

PROLOGUE

Lilacs were blooming in Cracauerplatz. The Visitor felt disoriented and alone, an outsider, lost without a map. Her atrophied German stuck in her throat. Thirty-one years had elapsed between her last stay in Germany (for an ill-fated job in Frankfurt) and her return to Berlin in late middle age. The city struck her as post-apocalyptic—flat and featureless except for its rivers, its lakes, its legions of bicyclists. She found herself nameless: nameless in crowds, nameless alone. Another disappearance in a city with a long history of disappearance acts.

The Visitor's arrival in late April wasn't auspicious. Her luggage was lost for two days. The skies remained overcast. Their vast bleakness heightened her malaise. The apartment in Charlottenburg, on the west side of Berlin, was exactly what she'd wanted: a white cube with nondescript furnishings and a bedroom barely big enough to sleep in. A modest balcony overlooked the Kaiserdamm. The U-bahn was a block away, as was the Lietzensee, a picturesque city lake. After all her careful planning, everything was as she expected except for this: her staggering loneliness.

Why had she come? It boiled down to a story A. told her when they'd first met, at a dinner in her honor at a central New Jersey university. A. was Cuban-American, like her, and a writer. He was fluent in German and a fan of Berlin, often spending lengthy sojourns there. A. mentioned that after the Wall fell, he managed to reconstitute his aristocratic grandmother's vintage Spanish library from the used books stalls near the Bode Museum. The Visitor was hopelessly intrigued.

The two friends spoke often of political upheavals and the displacements of war, of revolution, the unlikely bedfellows these produced—most specifically, the human fallout from Cuba's long association with the Soviet bloc. All the flotsam and detritus of history, like the Visitor's Cuban-Russian cousin, Vladimir—someone she'd never met—who was born to her maternal uncle's first marriage to a Muscovite engineer in the 1960s. It was stories like these that the Visitor hoped to find in Berlin.

But the initial clarity of her mission gave way to a paralyzing vagueness during her first days in the city. Was it the jet lag? The long pale nights that seemed to stretch endlessly to dawn? The moths bumping against her windows like insistent ghosts? The Germans' radiant disregard of her? Here she was just another hooded crow perched in a linden tree.

True, there was much weighing her down: the end of her second marriage to a cellist from Iowa; the final rupture from her vicious mother, whom she'd indecorously called madre de mierda on her way out the door. A backwash of memories she preferred to forget. She no longer had a home, or a homeland. She no longer had a mother, nor was she an active mother herself (her twenty-year-old daughter was happily studying in Barcelona). This was her life now: unoccupied, disconnected, alone, invisible. Somehow she'd imagined a grander liberation.

As *a child the Visitor had kept diaries, which her mother read during the brief interludes when she wasn't obsessing over her husband's infidelities. No matter that the Visitor (when little) had hidden the diaries under her mattress, or the lining of her winter coat. Before long, she retaliated by planting false stories, fantasizing about a life without her mother in it. She'd understood even then that her best self was her illicit self, the one that provoked the mother, the one the mother couldn't own. So, no, the Visitor decided, she wouldn't keep a journal in Berlin, or write about herself in the first person. Rather, she would indulge the luxury of a more distant perspective.*

Her wanderings in Berlin began tentatively, her encounters awkward and forced. The isolation felt physical, three-dimensionally oppressive, but it fueled a manic movement. The Visitor walked everywhere, often logging upward of ten miles a day. She explored the city, eavesdropped on conversations, walked off her anxiety, all the while lighting a match to her present, reminding herself that she was alive and free. More strenuously still, she signed up for a Zumba class with a former Olympian speed skater, then for water aerobics with octogenarians who left her gasping for air.

The Visitor returned again and again to the zoo, where she practiced her rusty German on the cheetahs and polar bears. To her surprise, she felt most at home in the aquarium. For hours she watched the lolling puffer fish with their bulging cartoon eyes. Officious iridescent taxi fish patrolled the perimeter, tap-tapping against the glass. There were stick insects and locusts, slugs, obese water snakes. The otherwise unremarkable "false map" turtles intrigued her with their evocative name. We're all exiles here, she thought.

On her twelfth day in Berlin, a young father asked the Visitor for directions in German, to which she correctly replied. A turning point. Soon she'd be talking to people in parks, at museums, along the Spree River, in the city's many acres of outdoor cafés. Thus, her mission began.

I

THE FLAMING COMMON

Helmut Bauer

MOTHS

By the end of World War II, 91 of the 3,715 animals at the Berlin Zoo had survived. These included two lions, an Asian bull elephant, a cackle of hyenas, a hippopotamus bull, ten hamadryas baboons, and a rare black stork. My father, Klaus Bauer, had been the zoo's last keeper before he was called off to war. This was after a severe firebombing had boiled alive the remaining crocodiles and tortoises at the aquarium, and a puma escaped through the flames, only to be shot by a frightened housewife in Lützowplatz. Opportunists benefited from the destruction, partook of crocodile-tail steaks and fashioned sausages from the charred bear meat. But the rats are what most thrived in Berlin.

Thank you for accompanying me this afternoon, Kind Visitor. I do enjoy a walk through the Tiergarten, even on drizzly days.

Once, I saw an old man club a duck to death with his cane at this very spot. It was just after the war, and, next to him, on a burnt-out tank, was a fly-poster advertising dance lessons. The times were extraordinary, rivaling anything I've ever read in books. The zoo is near here, in the southwestern corner of the park. I permit myself entrance every month or so—nobody bothers charging me—to visit the tropical aviaries and the lonely polar bears. Perhaps you've heard of the cub born in captivity here some years ago? Millions swarmed the zoo to get a glimpse of Baby Knut. Unfortunately, the poor creature collapsed and died after five short years.

Today, I promised to speak to you of my father, and so I shall. My earliest memories of him are at this zoo, where I helped him feed the animals on weekends. How he'd loved the antics of the cockatoos—*as cunning as our politicians*, he used to say—and the idiosyncrasies of Jupp, the elderly cheetah, who insisted on having his hindquarters scratched with a rake. It was from the cockatoos' aviary that Vati "borrowed" Miamor, a Cuban Amazon parrot, in order to save it from starvation. But in the commotion of an air raid, Miamor disappeared from our apartment, most likely for someone's dinner.

When the Reich drafted Vati for an army reserve battalion late in the war, he was arthritic and nearing fifty. You might say that my life—or the heart of it, anyway—stopped on the day he left. A peeling poster on our apartment building showed a woman and boy battling a fire with buckets of water. I pretended that they were Mutti and me, and dreamt about stealing a little wood gas car, too. In my fantasy, I drove us to safety, though I could barely ride a bicycle then. Most nights, we raced into the air-raid shelter, to the shrill sound of sirens. Mutti was profoundly deaf, the result of a childhood fever, and she was no longer pretty to anyone but me. As the bombs fell, she rubbed her sternum as if she were erasing a mistake. Sometimes I feared she'd erase herself altogether.

That winter, we watched the city camouflage itself with false treetops in raised netting and decoy buildings to deceive the British bombers. There were rumors of a fake capital being built to the north, but nobody had seen it. Rumors, Kind Visitor, were what we lived on. My friends and I played in the ruins, when we could, taking turns blowing on a beat-up trumpet we'd found. It was our greatest treasure. On the rare evening when there was no Verdunkle, my mother permitted me, against the rules, to light her incandescent lamp. Its hypnotizing hot wire drew an astonishing variety of moths to its flame.

One day my friend Kuno Schulz triumphantly brought home a hunk of horsemeat. Kriegsglück, everyone said, coveting a bloody piece. War luck. On another occasion, Kuno happened across a dead British pilot whose plane had crashed into a building off Nollendorfplatz. As a crowd cautiously gathered, Kuno stole away with the pilot's unopened parachute, a windfall of silk for his mother. Later, Frau Schulz bartered swaths of the silk with the other mothers as they busily converted their Nazi flags to Allied ones. Before long, these were hanging from what was left of their balconies.

In the last weeks of the war, Hitler Youth patrolled our neighborhood with rifles, and some of the older boys we knew rode rickety bicycles into battle with Panzerfausts attached to the handlebars. Of them, only Markus Achziger survived—but without his legs.

■

The day the Russians reached Berlin, my mother gave me a pair of my own unraveling socks embroidered with the number 9. I'd forgotten it was my birthday. For supper, Mutti and I ate nettles soup (though I dreamt every night of mashed potatoes sprinkled with crisp bacon) and prayed to God for mercy. In the final terrifying days of battle, my ordinarily meek mother joined a band of housewives who looted whatever they could. Never mind that such behavior was punishable by death. Kind Visitor, what once had been inconceivable became commonplace; grace and disgrace, one and the same.

I watched camels and shaggy Cossack ponies trudging down Unter den Linden. Russian infantrymen in tunics and fur caps rode gypsy wagons and phaetons and every manner of conveyance. People whispered that the Ivans were lighting campfires in the Reichstag—our Reichstag!—and violating women of all ages. Here, at last, were the savages we'd been taught to fear. That summer, the Americans arrived in their gleaming jeeps. How awestruck we were by the black GIs! We crowded around them for chocolates and chewing gum, which they handed out more freely than the other soldiers.

Miraculously, Vati returned home after the defeat. In our district, I was the only child with a living father. He and I toured what was left of the zoo: the burnt-out elephant house (where a bull had frantically trumpeted the coming doom); the scorched treetops where dozens of monkeys had perished. We spoke of the leopards and panthers, jaguars and apes that had escaped after a particularly bad raid, the snakes slithering through terrified crowds fleeing the fires and bombs. And yet, I felt lucky. Most of my surviving friends were raised by their widowed mothers. Those who'd lost both parents got by as best they could, digging through the rubble, fighting over scraps like wild dogs. Who knew what became of them? Even the savvy Kuno, with his Kriegsglück, disappeared without a trace. Knowing him, he probably ended up in your San Francisco driving a fancy Cadillac.

My father? Kind Visitor, you must understand that, once, Vati had been a man whose happiness had seemed to me as predictable as the sun. Upon his return, he fell into a catatonic state that was impervious even to Mutti's devoted ministrations. And the blisters on his feet, the ones he got from his long march home, never healed. Whatever hope we had soured to futility.

At his funeral in 1951, two members of his battalion showed up from Hamburg to pay their respects. Mutti insisted that I show them around the dilapidated zoo. To my surprise, one of the old lions was still alive and weakly roaring. The veterans drank and drank, shedding no light regarding their duties on the Eastern front. Instead they shook their heads dully and took turns clapping me on the back, repeating the same stock phrase: *Your father was an honorable man, the most honorable among us.*

Sometimes, Kind Visitor, I long to send letters to the past . . . but who would write back?

Ernesto Cuadra

KIDNAPPED

When I returned to Cuba after five months as a prisoner of war on a German submarine, nobody believed me. Everyone assumed that I'd run away with a girlfriend to Havana or gotten eaten by sharks. I'm telling you there was no trace of me except for Oscarito, my identical twin. Ay, but I see you're raising an eyebrow already. I'm not convincing you? A good story—and mine is true, I swear it—requires some tilling of the soil beforehand. You can't just throw a handful of seeds on the ground and expect anything to grow.

Let me try again. It was 1943, and I was the night watchman for an electric-fan factory on a beautiful stretch of Cuban coast—as far east as you can go on the island without falling into the ocean. It was late in May, and a bit hazy. The moon was lighting up the clouds, the air unusually still. I was alone guarding the factory, property of Dr. Faustino Buendía, who, with his eternal scowl, was neither a doctor nor ever had a good day in his life. I was sixteen and had just lost my virginity. Tío Eufemio had arranged it. He made it his business to "break in" all the Cuadra boys at a brothel in Baracoa. I felt proud to have gotten the night watchman job, too; even prouder when I was issued a pistol. En fin, I'd become a man.

Let me tell you that none of these accomplishments served me in the least when those German seamen approached while I dozed at my post. The mosquitoes had pestered me for the first hour of my shift, and then they, too, buzzed off to sleep. The German who woke me spoke a few words of Spanish and assured me they meant no harm. What they needed, he said, gesturing stiffly, were supplies for their vessel: ham, mangoes, coffee, butter, eggs. And, he asked, did I happen to have any rum? This didn't surprise me. Everyone knew that Cuba produced the best rum in the world. I blinked and rubbed my eyes. I wanted to remember this strange dream to tell Oscarito, who'd probably wave it away, saying, *Get to the point, Ernesto!* And as usual, I'd say, *Dreams don't have points, hermano!*

I told the leader—who introduced himself as Joachim Freyer— that I had two tins of sardines and a hunk of dried beef, which Mami had packed for my dinner. I was happy to share.

"No rum?" He looked crestfallen.

I'd gotten drunk only once—on the night of my visit to the brothel, in fact—but I was careful not to drink on the job. Dr. Buendía had warned, *If I catch you with booze, you're out of here!* In any case, I still believed I was dreaming, so when the Germans disarmed me, pointed their weapons at my chest, and demanded that I return with them to their submarine, I resisted.

"I can't go," I whined. "Mami will worry."

When Joachim translated my remarks to the other men, there were belly laughs all around, but nobody lowered their guns. And so—mi madre!—I was taken prisoner. As I said, I remained at sea for five months. It wasn't easy for me to adjust. My first days onboard I was green from seasickness and lurched around like a borracho. I banged my head on pipes, handwheels, bulkheads, you name it. The crew nicknamed me Bluterguss for all my bruises. The humidity, even for an islander like me, was intolerable. Everything was slimy, wet, moldy, including the food. I felt as if I were trapped in the neck of a bottle.

Soon my homesickness grew worse than my nausea. When I thought of Mami picking pebbles out of a colander of rice, or Oscarito staring up at the rafters from the small straw bed we'd shared, it was all I could do to hold back tears. I dreamt of papayas with lime, fried plantains, coconut ice cream. Once, I woke up to the croaking of Cuban tree frogs and had to shake my head free of the sound. And I swear, La Virgen de la Caridad del Cobre appeared to *me* on the stormy seas! Cuba was Germany's enemy, having sided with the Allies and harbored Jewish refugees. But nobody onboard held this against me.

■

Most of the crew wasn't much older than me, but they had long beards and stank like Señora Portuondo's backyard goats. Happily, they were glad for my company—clapping me on the back, shouting *Gut! Gut!* for any little thing I accomplished. Even dour Captain Wruck warmed up to me after a while. The U-boat patrolled the Eastern seaboard from Newfoundland to the Caribbean. To my surprise, the Germans regularly snuck ashore on enemy territory—Florida, Virginia, New York—to replenish their supplies and commit acts of sabotage. In July, they blew up an electrical plant on Long Island, and we watched the entire shoreline go dark except for the flames leaping to the skies. Another time, Joachim brought back a dozen stolen hams still warm from their smoking shed.

The submarine got as far north as the tip of Greenland, where we met up with a secret refueling tanker. The icebergs defied imagination—a flotilla of gleaming peaks of all sizes, drifting in the pale green waters, translucent under the twilit summer skies. How did this world exist on the same planet as Cuba?

■

A host of daily drills and maintenance tasks took up most of our waking hours. I became keenly interested in the fifty-ton storage batteries that kicked into gear whenever the vessel submerged (the hammering diesel engines operated when we surfaced, or when we were at periscope depth, which recharged the batteries). Tobias, the top mechanic, taught me everything he knew about the batteries. Reliable but highly toxic—they leaked poisonous chlorine fumes when damaged—the batteries were the submarine's lifeline as well as a deadly threat. One of the radio operators, Ulf, also took me under his wing and let me listen in on the hydrophone, which could capture the sound of a ship's propellers seventy miles away.

In the rare quiet hours, I learned to play chess and card games like Döppelkopf and Skat. I taught Ulf and Tobias basic Spanish and learned some German myself—a torturous language, if you ask me.

We had several close calls with British and American destroyers (our U-boat sank over fifty thousand tons of cargo while I was at sea)—not to mention a serious control-room fire. But nothing was so nerve-rattling as when the Allies began using twin-engine patrol bombers against us. The fact that enemy convoys now had their own air defense crushed the Germans' ideas of U-boat warfare—and sank dozens of their fleet. In no time, there was a cemetery of iron coffins on the ocean bottom. Nobody, least of all the captain, ever expected to be shouting *Flugzeug!* on the high seas and then crash-diving for cover.

During one particularly ferocious battle with a British warship, we were trapped for twenty-two hours at a near-hull-crushing depth of 280 meters. The steel shrieked, valves blew, deck plates jumped, and the boat was plunged into complete darkness. Bombs and depth charges detonated above us, sending shockwave after deafening shockwave. The bilges flooded and kept us ankle-deep in water, oil, and piss. Everyone was half-suffocated, shivering, sick with fear. Who knows how many Hail Marys I said? I'm telling you I could feel my heart beating under my tongue! As we waited, condemned, in our underwater tomb, I felt closer to death than to life. Créeme, it was a miracle we survived.

I suppose you could say it wasn't the worst adventure for a teenage boy. On my seventeenth birthday, the Germans got me good and drunk on what was left of their schnapps and failed miserably to sing the Cuban national anthem. As the war grew worse for them—the crew spoke openly of this, grounds for treason if they'd been found out—they agreed, at great risk to themselves, to drop me off back in Cuba instead of surrendering me as a prisoner of war. Had they been caught, every last man would've been executed, no questions asked.

Sí, I do believe that my allegiances shifted onboard—not for the Nazis, never—but for these good, brave men. Joachim, who became a lifelong friend, encouraged me to look him up in Berlin after the war. As a parting gift, he gave me his precious 7x50 Leitz binoculars.

■

Bueno, you can imagine my family's shock when I returned home, looking like a crazy jungle man. I was ten pounds thinner, too, and swaying on sea legs but otherwise none the worse for wear. As I told them the story of my capture, they laughed as if it were the funniest joke they'd ever heard. But when they saw I was dead serious—and rattled off German phrases as proof—they were convinced that I'd somehow knocked myself on the head and lost my memory. What other explanation could there be? Oscarito, who hated ambiguity and aimed his words straight as arrows, put an arm around my shoulders. "I don't give a damn what happened to you, hermano. I'm just glad to have you back."

What could I say? Sometimes the truth is so outlandish that it's better to let people believe you're indulging in fantasy.

The next Saturday, my parents threw me a welcome-home party and invited the whole neighborhood. They pit-roasted a pig in banana leaves, cooked vats of black beans and rice, and baked enough flan to make our teeth ache. Tío Eufemio hired the best conjunto in town to play the changüís and guarachas that kept us dancing long into the night. When the party wound down, I walked toward the sugar mill, where my family had slaved for decades. In this world of sugarcane, time had stood still for over a century, one season following the next with barely a change. I thought of the U-boat batteries, how they'd saved us time and again, how they might save Baracoa.

I finally did visit Joachim. Not right after the war—that was impossible—but in 1957, after I made a fortune in industrial batteries. I'd studied engineering and designed batteries that kept everything in the sugar mills—from the crusher rollers to the centrifuges—operating without gasoline, or costly interruptions. I sold my patents to manufacturers in Brazil, the Philippines, even the U.S. It was because of those Germans that I became a self-made millionaire, Cuba's king of batteries. Then the dichosa revolution happened and destroyed everything. I made a terrible mistake not leaving the island when I could.

Joachim married a Polish woman and had three daughters, one of them an albino. He looked more shrunken than he had on the submarine, probably due to the contrast in surroundings. Joachim taught Spanish—with a Cuban accent, imagínate tú—at a local high school and did so until his retirement. Now I'm here in Berlin for his funeral. Me? It took me forever to find a wife. I was almost fifty when I married a widow and adopted her six kids. I won over my Graciela with pink carnations. Cartloads of them. She didn't believe the story of my kidnapping either, though she was tolerant enough and enjoyed my guttural impersonations of the crew. By then, I'd long stopped caring what people thought.

Let me tell you something else: I'm the exact same age as Fidel himself. We were born just two days and thirty miles apart in 1926. I hang on, praying he'll go first. At home in Baracoa, I like to sit on my veranda at night, especially when the moon is full, and scan the horizon with my German binoculars. My wicker swing overlooks the sea, and sometimes I imagine that German submarine rising up out of the Caribbean, coming for me once more. But this time, amiga, I wouldn't hesitate. I would willingly go.

Sophie Echt

TOMB

I was buried in a church graveyard for thirty-seven days but wasn't dead myself. Not buried exactly but ensconced in a sarcophagus, the contents of which had been disposed of by my husband. This happened in the middle of the war. Now it is I who am burying my beloved Uwe in the same churchyard cemetery where he'd hidden me. I'm not sure where to begin, my dear. If there's anything I've learned from studying Russian literature, it's that you can't rush a story.

The sarcophagus belonged to W. F., a coal magnate who'd designed and erected his final resting place while still in his thirties (he died at seventy-nine). Fortunately for me, W. F. had been a giant of a man and built his marble tomb to match. Four men of average stature could've rested in its confines quite comfortably.

Even so, how could I have imagined sleeping inside it for a single night, much less inhabiting it for over a month? It was late in the spring of 1942. My husband had the good sense not to propose his plan ahead of time. Instead he presented it to me as a fait accompli.

I'd managed to stay enrolled at the university—nobody yet knew of my Jewish grandmother—though the Reich frowned upon advanced education for women. The goal for German women then? To become baby factories for the Fatherland. I, however, concentrated on my doctoral thesis, which analyzed the hypocrisies of social class in Ivan Goncharov's nineteenth-century comic masterpiece, *Oblomov*. But when Germany attacked the Soviet Union the previous summer, all Russian-related research—scientific, political, and literary—came to a halt.

My husband saw the portents long before I did and busily prepared the sarcophagus. He'd been fretting over the intensity of the purges at the university, had heard rumors of labor camps and massacres in the forests of Poland. When I thought Uwe was in the library studying for his medical exams, it turned out he was chiseling air holes in the tomb through which he expected me to breathe. He furnished it with what he could—a flashlight, moldering pillows, a woolen blanket, books of Russian poetry (Akhmatova, Mandelstam, Tsvetaeva), assorted comestibles (sausages, Volkenbrot, chocolate), and a tin waste pail.

When at last Uwe showed off my new quarters as if it were a cozy cottage, I cried, "Have you gone mad?" The next hours were impossible for him as he tried to bring me to my senses. My husband was a reliably rational, unflappable man—he later became a neurosurgeon of some renown—but as daylight broke and I still refused to hide in W. F.'s sarcophagus, he threatened to kill himself. Only then did I climb into the bone-chilling tomb.

Uwe promised to visit me every evening under the pretext of walking Friedl, a plump ball of fluff we'd inherited from our deceased neighbor next door. My husband brought me the day's news, urging me to remain calm while he arranged our transit out of the country (to England, he hoped, where he had professional contacts). To stray bystanders it would appear that Uwe was talking to the dog, which dutifully held up its paw for scraps. Two days after my "burial," the authorities came looking for me. Uwe told them that I'd fled without warning.

That first night in the sarcophagus was the longest of my life. My lungs burned for oxygen as I traced every centimeter of the tomb with my fingertips. Though I shivered, my skin felt scorched. I tasted the burial dirt. The cries of nocturnal birds tormented me. Better to die running, I thought, than like a rat in this hole. Had I been strong enough to push aside the marble lid (reading novels, even Russian ones, hadn't prepared me for this), I would have tried to, but Uwe, in his genius, had secured it from the outside.

By the time my husband returned the following evening, I was hysterical. "Shoot me!" I begged. "If you love me, kill me!" But he refused to open the tomb or remove my waste. Rightly, he calculated, it would take me several days to settle in.

The second night was worse than the first. The stink was asphyxiating; time an incalculable weight around my neck. The trees soughed without diction or pity. The bones of the dead mocked me. Try as I might, I couldn't focus long enough to read more than a line or two of poetry. What did poetry solve, I thought bitterly, when Hitler was annihilating the Jews? Action was what the world needed—warriors, not the wrecking balls of words.

When my husband opened the sarcophagus on the third evening, the rush of air overwhelmed me. I tried to escape, but my legs buckled. My clothes reeked as if I'd been living in the woods all winter. I sobbed, dazzled by the immensity of the starry skies. Uwe spoke to me as if I were a child, rocking me in his arms. "A few more weeks," he whispered. "Isn't that worth it to spend the rest of our lives together?"

By the fifth day, my anguish began to subside, and I forced myself to tackle one modest task after another. I pulled my hair back like a rope. Stooped over my flashlight, I memorized Akhmatova's poems, translating them into German in my head. *Twenty-first. Night. Monday.* / *Silhouette of the capitol in darkness.* / *Some good-for-nothing—who knows why—* / *made up the tale that love exists on earth.*

■

My dear, I grew well acquainted with my elemental self. The dimming of my eyesight heightened my other senses. The feathers in my pillow felt familiar, as if I myself had coaxed the geese into relinquishing them. Tightly wrapped in my blanket, I pictured the bleating sheep as they, too, surrendered their wool. I dreamt of trees and their skyward branches; the tangled rhizomes of nameless plants. In that icy marble lung of a tomb, I rationed my breath until it appeared as diaphanous as a veil. When I found it impossible to sleep, I pressed my lips to the air holes, sucking what I could from the spring.

Toward the end of my entombment (though I didn't know then it was nearly over), I woke up to find a grass snake stretched out against my leg. It was my sole company for two days. I suspected something dreadful had befallen my husband and grew frantic with worry. I scratched at the tomb's walls until my fingertips bled, knocked my head against its unyielding marble, anything to stop my thinking. The little snake wound itself around my ankles, first one then the other, gazing at me for hours with a calming, hypnotic air.

When Uwe reappeared, he was hobbling on a broken leg (the result of a bad fall off a trolley). Cheerfully, he offered me a basket of strawberries and some Pfefferkäse and, though it was already night, we picnicked under a linden tree. Then I coaxed him back into the sarcophagus with me. No matter his injury, my hunger, our fears—we made love as if for the last time. The very next day, our passage to England came through, and we escaped.

Our journey? Ah, my dear, that's a story for another day. Suffice it to say that time changed us. Compromises defined us. Even devotion can wane then return with an unexpected ferocity. My darling Uwe succumbed to two affairs during our long marriage. Betrayal? No, no, no. I quickly forgave him both transgressions. It was the least I could do for saving our lives.

Anna Wildgrube
CRIMINALS

Si vis pacem, para bellum.

When the ophthalmologist took a look at my cataracts and suggested lens implants, I said: *I've seen too much as it is.* Dr. Alves shrugged but said nothing more. Show me the surgeon today who has five minutes to spare for an old woman like me. But who am I to complain? The clock was my master, too, until I retired. Criminals paid dearly for my time—very dearly—to spare themselves public humiliation. Ach, such sporadic bursts of faux guilt and atonements.

Back in the day, there were next to no women in my line of work. The courtroom was a sea of men in sober suits. The trials of retribution from World War II went on for decades, beginning with the Spruchkammern and the ineffectual denazification courts. Incidentally, the Fragebogen—the Allies' postwar questionnaire—was a joke. Who in their right mind would willingly admit complicity? In wartime everyone knew that if you stopped for mercy, you were as good as dead.

There's no perfect crime, I used to tell my clients. *But there is such a thing as a perfect defense.* No matter how egregious their offenses, if I could demonstrate to the court that the accused were part of a larger flow of history for which they weren't individually responsible, acquittals were certain. What did I argue? Essentially this: that a cog is not the machine. Dear Visitor, history can't be erased, but it is definitely subject to negotiation. What did I instruct my clients to say? *I was following orders. I was on furlough then. The Jews were all gone by the time I arrived. I knew nothing about that.* Und so weiter. I lose nothing by telling you this now. So few of those who might still be tried are alive.

■

I grew up in Spandau, a nondescript suburb west of Berlin. Our sole claim to fame was that Frau Beckmann, our next-door neighbor, won the Mother of the Year Award in '38 for giving birth to healthy quintuplets. A dazed Frau Beckmann was interviewed on the radio, and the Führer himself presented her with a medal for *exemplary service to the Fatherland.* Her oldest daughter, Frieda, was my best friend, and so I got to hold her mother's medal, imagining the glory that could be mine. The Führer took a special interest in birthrates and marriages in those days, presenting Nazi newlyweds with a special wedding edition of *Mein Kampf.*

More specifically? Well, I remember a schoolyard fight between two "Aryans" and a Jewish girl early in the war. When the Jewish girl got the best of her attackers, they were incredulous:

"You can't fight back! You're a Jew!" Soon afterward the girl and her family vanished. Neighbors squabbled over the furniture left behind in their apartment. That same winter, our school received shipments of coats and jackets from the Eastern front along with boots, cuckoo clocks, frying pans, blankets, candelabras. One of my classmate's fathers was SS, and his family got first pick of the loot. His wife snapped up a chinchilla wrap, which she took to showing off, sparking the jealousy of the other mothers.

My father had a jewelry kiosk near the Hauptbahnhof, which, except for selling cheap wedding rings to soldiers leaving for the front, was going out of business. Vati grew increasingly morose and paranoid. Some days it took all his effort to get out of bed, even with his Pervitin, to which he became severely addicted. Then he visited a hypnotist, who advised him to drink water with rose syrup (an unheard-of luxury at the time), but Vati went bankrupt just the same. Though he wasn't old, his lungs were weak from childhood asthma, and he succumbed to pneumonia in the winter of '44.

My life, and Mutti's, got a lot harder. We took turns queuing up at the water pump and stepped over the growing number of corpses in Hermannplatz. One happy day, we feasted on a tinned ham we'd found in a bombed-out flat. In the cellar where we hid when the bombs dropped, the jokes grew grimmer. *Better a Russki on the belly than an Ami on the head.* Everyone wrung their hands, preparing for the worst. The anxious strain drove many to kill themselves rather than wait for the end. As Berlin fell, the weather turned warm and beautiful. *Führer weather*, people used to say. The lilacs were defiantly in bloom. Dragonflies darted through the air with a blue magic. Since when does nature stop for war?

When it was over—how disoriented we were by the sudden quiet—new troubles began. Around us the city lay in ruins, like the photographs of archaeological sites I'd seen in history books. We had the complexion of corpses ourselves from living underground. I saw buildings split in two, cross sections of their interiors visible. Twisted pipes jutted every which way from the rubble.

Dear Visitor, the world we knew was over. There were only two religions: hunger, and the relief thereof. Of course, one could also mail twenty marks to a soothsayer in Bavaria to divine the future, but of what use was that? The Brandenburg Gate became ground zero for the black market: fur coats, diamonds, antiques, binoculars, watches. Anything and everything. I saw babies given away more than once. The principal currencies, however, remained constant: cigarettes and sex.

The Russians went after the fat women first, which meant the wives of Nazi Party men—the Frau Sowiesos with their noses in the air. But no female, young or old, was safe. *Frau komm!* Every woman dreaded those words. Mothers pointed out other girls' hiding places to protect their own. Imagine, if you will, the moment before enemy soldiers rape your daughter. Women asked each other: *How many times?* Then they turned away.

It was a Russian officer who took Mutti and me under his wing. *Ptiska*, he called me, Little Bird, as he caressed my torn woolen sweater. I was barely fourteen. Frightful, I know, but I was luckier than most. For the price of an irregular, temporal domesticity, that lieutenant saved our lives with butter, bacon, and bread.

When the Americans arrived that summer, a few of us took up with the black GIs. They flashed their hands in double V's and softened our names on their tongues. Later, the babies came, a bumper crop of Besatzungskinder. I was lucky I didn't get pregnant.

■

What can I tell you after decades defending my clients? The irony, Dear Visitor, is that the victims had a much harder time proving their innocence than did the guilty, who frequently escaped prosecution with a well-paid "witness" or two. I'm retired now, drawing a pension, but the denunciations against me don't stop. Stimmt. I've been accused of sheltering murderers with legal jargon and technicalities. But what would've happened if we'd permitted our society to unravel? Every family afflicted, pinned to the past like insects. How could we have built a new future like that?

Believe me, Dear Visitor, it would've been much easier for me, for anyone, to defend the victims. But the perpetrators? Who wanted to look in the mirror, at that beckoning finger, and see the possibility in themselves?

SPY

Be sure to change my name and all identifying details, got that? I don't want anyone recognizing me. By the time this sees the light of day—*if* it sees the light of day—I'll be dead. I'd be lucky to last another month in this hole. Not too many people know about it. How'd you find it, anyway? That's right, my friend, they should rename it the Erich Mielke Nursing Home for Ex-Stasi. It used to be our cathouse, but you probably know that already.

In the old days I would've known your game by now. Espionage, blackmail, you name it—we were the best. So good that our citizens did most of the work for us. That's how afraid we had them. But who admits to having worked for Die Firma nowadays? To hear people talk, nobody was an informant. Nobody got his hands dirty. Hell, nobody in this whole fucking country ever took so much as a dump! I see you've done your homework. Good for you, my friend, good for you. Yes, I did train Cuban agents for a time—entrapment, extortion, anything embarrassing, as if you people could be embarrassed by anything.

Richtig. It was a Cuban who nailed me. Hércules was his name. How could I make this shit up? As good-looking and seductive as his name. I wasn't bad-looking myself in those days, but this guy was in a league by himself. He wooed men and women with equal ease. A real player. Never looked back either. You won't believe me but I'm telling you that I was a happily married man with four teen-aged sons at the time. What I *didn't* know? That I was being set up.

Why? Because the motherfuckers had nothing on me. You've got to understand that agents like me were constantly being tested with bribes, liquor, hustlers, drugs. Some of us were addicted to Valium, painkillers, other crap. But here's the rub: you only got promoted when they had you by the balls. That's how they ensured your loyalty on the way up. Except, stupidly, I didn't think it could ever happen to me.

My boss invited me into his office to watch the video they'd taken. Sadistic bastard. I never sweated so much in my life. He offered me a deal: go to jail, or I, family man and loyal Stasi agent, could "choose" to become a homosexual decoy, recruiting foreign informants. I'd travel abroad, get a generous raise, screw the men (and a few women) I was told to screw, and obtain the necessary information. The luxuries I'd bring home from these trips would make life more bearable for my wife and the boys.

Eleven years I did this. Until the Wall came down. Like an idiot, I fell for another Cuban, a colonel who'd been on assignment in Angola—no names!—but trust me, I screwed him over just the same. Call it payback. My sons went to university and moved on to white-collar jobs. My wife never found out. Condoms? How could I have explained that to her? She died of cervical cancer in 1991, probably from some disease I gave her. Bertha died thinking I'd been the perfect husband—faithful, hardworking, an upstanding Communist. All the while, I was screwing men on three continents.

How did I do it? The way most people do despicable things: by not thinking about it, separating it from the rest of my life. That's right, compartmentalizing. I was good at my job. I've always been competitive. What the fuck! Are you crazy? Why the hell would I have kept photographs? I destroyed everything when the time came. Look, you better not use my real name, or you'll regret it. I may be old and sick, but I still have friends I can call on. Remember, *you* used to be the enemy. *Truth* was the enemy. But no longer, my friend, no longer.

Christine Meckel

NURSE

To dying soldiers night comes beckoning . . .

—GEORG TRAKL

My real name is Christine Meckel and I was a young, inexperienced nurse when I arrived in V——, in the conquered Soviet territories. I'd graduated from an accelerated nursing program that provided medical support to our soldiers on the Eastern front. The Führer hailed it as an opportunity to participate in the grand expansion of the Reich, a solution to what he called our status as a Volk ohne Raum.

I grew up the second youngest in a large Catholic family in Berlin. When I got pregnant at sixteen—by a friend of my father's, a married man with a daughter my own age—the disgrace was unbearable. My parents shipped me off to a convent in the countryside that took in unwed mothers. There was no question that I'd have to give up the baby for adoption. I caught only a glimpse of my boy before he was taken away from me. Then I was put to work at the same Catholic hospital, emptying bedpans and scrubbing floors.

The war was in full swing. The Führer spoke of restoring Germany to its former glory, before the Great War had brought the country to its knees. It was this humiliation that Germans had trouble swallowing. Our pride, Liebe, is both our best asset and worst trait. When I learned that I could serve the Reich as a nurse and move far away, I jumped at the chance. Not for political reasons, please understand, but for personal ones. My nerves were steady and I didn't flinch at the sight of blood. Besides, I'd already committed a mortal sin. What more did I have to fear?

It took eight days of interrupted train travel to reach the remote town of V——, where I joined a reserve of nurses under our supervisor, Lotte Raeber. I lived in barracks, slept on a cot, stored my belongings in a metal locker. Nurse Raeber kept us to a punishing schedule. Days began with predawn rounds and frequently ended past midnight. If we were awake, we were working. Two buildings made up the clinic—one for our soldiers; the other for ethnic German civilians. No Jews were permitted in either, nor were Slavs. Both were considered "subhumans" and "useless eaters," Untermenschen who must be put to work, or to death.

As a nurse recruit, I quickly learned that our mission was less to heal life than to dispense with it. In V——, the sick were considered a burden, as were the old, the mentally incompetent, and the whining orphans—all problems with a single solution. No case, Nurse Raeber instructed us, was too insubstantial to "resolve." She filled our aprons with syringes of morphine and barbiturates and took extra pleasure in dispatching the complainers. We were so busy that I barely had time to reflect on what was becoming routine. I know how that sounds, Liebe, but the truth was that I steeled myself daily to do my job and not question it.

My worst memory? Bitte, allow me to close my eyes for a moment. This is difficult for me, like swallowing fishhooks. Ja, I remember a pair of teenagers I helped pry apart so that Nurse Raeber could inject them with deadly doses of morphine. They clung to each other frantically, vowing their undying love. How the winter winds blew when Nurse Raeber and I disposed of their stiffening bodies on the frozen pile of corpses outside. I was accustomed to the bitter cold in Berlin, but it was nothing compared to the depths of winter in Russia. So this was to be our new Lebensraum, I asked myself, our Garden of Eden?

Wounded soldiers, in their delirium, often mistook me for an angel and asked me for blessings, or forgiveness. What jolted their nerves most? The killing of children, typically by smashing their skulls against tree trunks. Other soldiers begged me for a kiss, or my hand in marriage, or to peer under their bandages and inventory the losses: eyes, abdomen, manhood, feet. I did my best to soothe them, to hold their mangled hands, to listen to their deathbed confessions. A few anguished ones pleaded for mirrors, but this was strictly forbidden. I reassured them with our unvarying script: that they'd fought valiantly for the Fatherland; that their suffering hadn't been in vain; that they'd soon return home to their sweethearts and families, who'd love them all the more for their sacrifices.

Of course these were lies, but what choice did I have? Whom or what would I be serving by telling them the truth? I'd venture to say that these lies—or rather, the relief these lies brought—probably saved me from losing my mind altogether.

■

After barely a year in V——, the Russians forced us into a chaotic retreat. Nurse Raeber called a staff meeting and required us to take an oath of secrecy. Then she issued new orders. Our blind, mutilated, brain-damaged soldiers were to be "relieved" of their misery. There were euphemisms for everything in those days—so much fancy language for unfancy murder. The edict, Nurse Raeber emphasized, had come from the "highest level," which meant Himmler, or even the Führer himself. There would be no trains to take our soldiers home, no hospitals to care for them any longer. In war, only the able-bodied could survive.

I know, Liebe, I know. You won't find evidence of this in any history books, but I'm telling you, it happened.

None of the nurses kept in touch after the war. This wasn't advisable, particularly once the investigations began. Sometimes I wonder what happened to Winfried L., the timid girl from Wiesbaden, who read Russian novels by flashlight, or the cheerful Heike P., who baked us strudels plump with summer berries, despite the shortage of flour. The only nurse I heard about later was the least trustworthy—Irmtraud K., who'd been mistress to the district commissar, ever preening in his mustard yellow uniform. In the 1960s, Irmtraud was summoned before a war crimes court and quoted in the newspapers as saying she couldn't remember whether she and the commissar had shot at deer, or fleeing Jews, in the woods. By then Irmtraud had become a social worker. I believe this was what saved her. Such "good" professions often mitigated the accused's original crimes.

My return to Berlin? I promise to continue the tale on your next visit, Liebe. I'm too weary now from telling you this much.

Did I mention that the center of my vision is worsening? As I look at your face, your features are missing. All I can discern are your hair and a bit of your jawline, a sliver of your sunburnt neck. As we gaze out at these gardens, only the edges of the flowerbeds are visible. Na ja, the world is vanishing around me.

My eye doctor says that macular degeneration is common at my age. Sadly, reading is an impossibility. Like Winfried, I used to enjoy Russian novels, though I remain partial to the British ones—*A Passage to India*, and so on. Now I'm reduced to listening to the evening news on television, though I don't set store by anything I hear. This weekend we'll be celebrating the hundredth birthday of a resident down the hall. Yesterday the gentleman addressed me formally in Russian. How did he know I would understand him?

The nursing home staffers cheerfully lie to us about everything, vital or not. Their lies are well-meaning, but they are lies nonetheless. No, Liebe, I don't begrudge them their lies. I suppose it's not the worst thing in the world to be treated as a child. After all, only children tell the truth—for a brief time, anyway—and people like me, who have nothing left to lose.

Every morning, I look in the mirror and see darkness where my face should be. Is there any greater freedom than that?

Horst Galbrech

DANCE CRAZE

Years ago as a minor official in the Ministry of Culture, I was ordered to come up with a dance craze to rival those convulsing the West—the twist, the pony, the baffling mashed potato. Because I'd once halfheartedly waltzed at a ministry holiday party, I was put in charge of this project. My superiors expected me to produce a miracle in three months, or, they intimated, heads would roll. I suspected a trick. After a generation of Soviet domination, East Germans were hardly renowned for being footloose. Marching in parade formation? Yes. Lining up for endless queues and shuffling forward? Absolutely. Suffering the requisite dances with elderly relatives at weddings? Awkwardly, but yes.

But to ask us to move our bodies, to shake and shimmy with abandon, to pop our joints and swing our fatty hips until all semblance of rectitude was gone? Mein Gott! The prospect was an unmitigated horror. It might've been the sixties everywhere else, but in the GDR, we were cultural hostages to the Cold War. Our country was woefully behind on all fronts, not the least of which was the radicalization of our disaffected youth. My superiors were determined to give the West a (managed) run for its money. To make my task all the more daunting, the new dance was to be free of suggestive movements—ignoring that eroticism was something of a national pastime. The Party was one thing; the people another. Yet anything remotely lascivious, my boss warned, would be deemed harmful to the morals of East German youth and exceedingly hazardous to my career. Ach, I lost many nights of sleep over this nonsense!

My wife, kind soul that she was, offered to help. Before long, it seemed that Sigrid had been waiting our entire married lives for the chance to undulate half-naked before me, provocations that flushed me pink to the tips of my ears. Who knew that she was capable of such indecency? My Sigrid enjoyed herself so thoroughly that her wrigglings led us to unprecedented bouts of amorousness. I began to think that my superiors had been correct when they'd cautioned me about the perils of unfettered dancing. After many infertile years, Sigrid and I conceived our first child on one frolicsome night. At the advanced age of forty-four, my wife gave birth to our beloved Hänschen.

But I digress—do forgive me, Dear Visitor.

■

So there I was, entrusted to invent a dance craze out of thin air, while keeping our young Communists pure of mind and body. I had to come up with a catchy name for it, too. Up until then

I'd been considered a bright, if flickering, light in the Ministry of Culture (my proposal on personal grooming workshops for Young Pioneers had been dismissed as perilously bourgeois). My reputation, meager as it was, rested on devising programs to keep our youth out of trouble and gainfully occupied—learning marksmanship, wood carving, and decorative egg painting, to name just a few. This dance business, I feared, could sabotage what remained of my dully graying career.

I consulted, discreetly, individuals in the demimonde of East Berlin (overrun by Stasi agents, I quickly learned), as well as foreign students, and emissaries from countries known for their tropical sensuality: Brazil, Cuba, and a few left-leaning African nations. One striking diplomat from Havana, a double agent known as Tania Tania, was sympathetic to my plight and agreed to privately demonstrate an unexpurgated mambo. Dear Visitor, I nearly fainted watching her gyrations.

"Can you do that without moving your hips?" I stammered, gasping for breath.

"Can you chew your food without teeth?" she snapped back.

I pulled a handkerchief from my jacket pocket and limply mopped my brow.

Then the Cuban agent offered to tutor me—and she said what follows with the seductive bluntness I've since come to associate with citizens of your island: *Now keep watching until you can suck the marrow from my bones.*

Achso.

Mustering my courage, I tentatively included a basic mambo variation in my proposed dance craze.

None of my superiors could make heads or tails of it. My attempts at breaking down the movements—I'd practiced them until

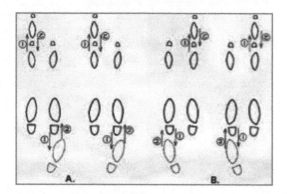

my feet blistered—made me look, in the words of one coworker, "like a malfunctioning propeller." Dispirited but undefeated, I decided, with the help of our desultory graphics department, to work up a more complex diagrammatic of exemplary, flexible, and—for a whiff of exoticism—dark-skinned youth.

After weeks of trial and error, I had my dance. The name I came up with—as if drawn like a rib from my side, I swear it—was the coup de grace: ISATSI! It had a wildly primal feel to it, yet my superiors at the Ministry of Culture couldn't help but notice that the letters, rearranged with the addition of an extra *i*, spelled Stasi. The dance, if I may be so immodest to suggest, evoked a certain foreign hedonism while paying homage to the most feared institution in the country. Capitalizing the name and adding a de rigueur exclamation point underscored the enthusiasm I hoped to ignite.

The music? I daresay it was something of a shotgun wedding between the mambo and the twist, with a touch of bossanova thrown in. At its unveiling before the top brass, the ISATSI! was met with universal approval—a rarity, trust me—and speedily given the go-ahead. In the somber corridors of the Ministry of Culture, once-dour colleagues clapped me on the back, winked at me with complicity, even envy. My hopes soared two octaves. For a time, I took to wearing a black beret at home. Its rakish angle inflamed my wife to ever more connubial delights. In a spirit of solidarity, Sigrid insisted that we dance the ISATSI! together every night, which naturally led to further erotic mischief.

The most difficult challenge proved to be piqueing the interest of the GDR's indifferent youth. The students, forcibly assembled in high schools in and around East Berlin, exhibited little to no curiosity in the ISATSI! Dear Visitor, there's no way to sugarcoat this: our large-scale dance lessons were abject failures. When I distributed the worksheets, most of the teens lowered their heads or slunk away in boredom. One or two jokingly shifted back and forth like rusty hinges. I wondered if their rigidity was due to their constraining uniforms, or to the inhibitions drummed into them by their teachers. Certainly it was not what I, or the Ministry of Culture, had intended.

You must believe me when I say that I tried everything possible to salvage my ISATSI! At one point I threw in a hard-charging polka backbeat, hoping this might stir the teens, but their impassivity proved impenetrable. Desperate, I zeroed in on Potsdam's sole performing arts school. Bullhorn in hand, I announced that the reward for those who danced for the song's duration was a free trip to a popular amusement park which featured, among its oxidized ruins, a mechanical Tyrannosaurus rex. Well, that did it. Instantly, the teens flooded the gymnasium floor and danced like it was the last party on earth.

After careful assessment, I pulled aside a dozen of the most physically coordinated and promised each of them a pair of bell-bottom jeans—Czech-made, but better than nothing—for participating in my pilot project. Dear Visitor, they leapt at the chance.

■

The Ministry of Culture scheduled our premiere for a Sunday night, in the prime spot immediately preceding the movie hour. As the much-anticipated day approached, there was a surfeit of optimism in our hallways. Backstage at the Deutsches Theater on Schumannstraße, makeup artists painted daisies and peace signs on our performers' cheeks while I fantasized about a big promotion, vacations to the Black Sea, a new refrigerator with a compartment for all the kilos of off-ration pork chops I'd be buying. Here, before an illustrious audience of the GDR's elite, was our answer to the Beatles and the Rolling Stones, to Elvis's hip-swiveling decadence. I felt confident that the ISATSI! would conquer them all.

At last the curtains parted and our black-market psyche-delic lights sputtered to life. The Potsdam teens, glittering in their costumes and flower-power makeup, stormed the stage and launched into their routine, twisting and clapping and jumping in syncopation. I surveyed the audience—highly decorated generals, ministers, and other top officials, including the head of the Stasi himself, Erich Mielke, who was seated with his family. Dear Visitor, not a single person so much as cracked a smile. The students were dancing their hearts out, but even their own parents were too frightened to react.

Mercifully, it was over in four minutes and thirty-two seconds. The teens stood hand in hand across the stage and bowed deeply, as we'd rehearsed. The silence lingered for an interminable moment. I sat there like an emptied glove, expecting the worse, now imagining myself chiseling stones in Siberia for an eternity. It was Mielke's adopted daughter who clapped first, startling those around her. Her father followed suit, icily staring straight ahead. Then the crowd burst into applause, whistling and thunderously stomping their feet, as if to compensate for their delayed response. The ISATSI! was a success!

That night, my wife and I celebrated with more dancing and a bottle of Bulgarian Sekt.

■

I'm an old man now, nearing ninety. The Berlin Wall, which had defined our lives for so long, was torn down, and the world we'd known changed forever. I was already retired and drawing a modest pension, which the West Germans graciously honored. My dear wife passed away on the eve of the new millenium, and our son, Hänschen, turned his back on GDR values and became a rich banker in London. Now and then I like to switch on the oldies radio station and pretend to dance with my frisky Sigrid again, inhaling the fragrance of her tousled hair.

Dear Visitor, how I wish I could report that the ISATSI! took the Soviet bloc by storm. But after the initial fanfare, my dance ended up where it probably belonged all along: in oblivion. Only I live to remember those halcyon days, the most golden of my career, and to share them with you today.

II

INVISIBLE BODIES

I would like to write as if I had remained silent.

—JÁNOS PILINSZKY

THE VISITOR

Her friend A. came to see the Visitor in Berlin. He wanted to show her "his" city: its histories and excavations, its uneasy embrace of the frayed eastern districts. Together they traveled to Karlshorst, where the German Armed Forces surrendered on May 8, 1945. For a mild-mannered man—A. would've been at home in a Kafka story—he knew all about the T-34 tank in the garden. Late afternoons, they devoured enormous slices of Erdbeerkuchen—strawberries were gloriously in season—and spiritedly fought over the bills.

The Visitor's German was improving day by day, and A. complimented her on her accent (his was flawless). Until then they'd spoken to each other only in English or Spanish, or a mix thereof. She recounted to him her three student summers in Germany. One year she'd lived in a commune of Marxist hippies in Freiburg. A copy of Das Kapital *sat on the toilet tank. Everyone slept with one another, but she demurred. Another summer in Münster, she'd watched a ragtag parade of veterans in their old Wehrmacht uniforms march by her host family's house.*

Later, the Visitor worked for an American firm in Frankfurt marketing disposable diapers. She bought a used Russian Lada that never worked. Her lies began almost immediately: that she'd studied literature in college; that she'd written her thesis on Joyce's Ulysses; *that she lived, above all, for poetry. One smitten colleague left chocolates on her desk. She slept with two of her coworkers: the Brit in hand soaps, and the Swiss intern in detergents. She played table tennis naked at a local spa. After six weeks, she quit the job, fleeing her thicket of lies. She resold the Lada to the same dealer for less than what she'd paid for it.*

The Visitor and A. spent hours at the three-story international bookstore on Friedrichstraße. There the Visitor learned that Hitler's gifts to Eva Braun had improved over the years. In 1937, he'd given her a book on Egyptian tombs for Christmas. Seven years later—a month before their marriage-suicide pact in the Führerbunker—he surprised her with a silver fox fur cape. Apparently, he'd avoided getting married before so as not to discourage German women from dreaming that, one day, he might be theirs.

The Visitor hadn't been lucky in love. But happy and unhappy seemed to her meaningless distinctions now. What mattered was this: Did the hardships get her to where she wanted to go? In contrast, A. had been gratefully (his word) married to the same German woman for twenty years. Her family hailed from Hoyerswerda and never forgave A. for taking their daughter away. They called him "the Negro" and "the Mexican" and once sang the Horst Wessel Song in his presence.

"The family is a police state," the Visitor said, describing how miniscule stages lit up inside her, repeating key scenes from her life. "Do people remember only what they can endure, or distort memories until they can endure them?"

After a long silence, A. said: "Childhood is a city you never leave. In Berlin's past, we seek our own." He believed that the tiniest crack in a random window could link one world to another. Then he held up a coffee-table book on Bauhaus style. "Only things endure."

The two discussed translations at length, as well as the untranslatable. They tried to render "Me duele una mujer" into another language. After failing miserably, they treated each other with even more tenderness than usual, as if to acknowledge the inadequacy of words. The Visitor had nick-named A. "jicotea," after he'd once described his dancing style as resembling "a turtle fighting its way out of a paper bag."

A perennial subject for them: their unbearable mothers, whom, they joked, had been separated at birth in Havana. Why, they wondered, had their mothers' particular sufferings and dislocations left them so indifferent to the misfortunes of others? So inflated about their self-worth? So violent?

In the Visitor's childhood home, dissent wasn't permitted; the daily temperature was set by her mother's rages. As a girl, her resistance had bloomed stealthily. She grew duplicitous, calculative, split herself to survive. Her public self was agreeable, loyal to a fault. All the while her private self was growing cutthroat, one eye on the exit, a Molotov cocktail in each hand. She told A. that she'd had to become a little monstrous to survive.

A. asked the Visitor if she planned to include her personal history alongside the stories she was collecting and retelling in Berlin. Everything that obsessed her, she insisted, was autobiographical in the extreme.

"Have you noticed," the Visitor said, changing the subject, "how the SS drumbeat sounds a lot like the clave?" It was another drizzly morning, and they were at the cemetery for Russian soldiers who'd died in the final assault on Berlin.

"Carajo." A. rarely cursed. "We always repeat what hurts us."

The Visitor surveyed the sea of tombstones, each with its pitifully inad-equate synopses. The shadows looked rinsed in the weak light.

"Not everyone who dies finds rest," A. said.

On their last afternoon together, the two ducked into a Brazilian bar off the Nollendorfplatz to wait out a thunderstorm. As the samba music played, A. told the Visitor tales about the Blue Division of the SS, its ranks filled with veteran Spanish soldiers, how they'd fought in the Reichstag to the bloody end. The two made a pact to write overlapping stories about them.

That night, they attended the Philharmonic to hear Bruckner's Symphony No. 7. Sixty-eight years earlier, a recording of its adagio was broadcast on Radio Berlin after Admiral Dönitz's address to the nation. Hitler has fallen, Dönitz announced, fighting to his last breath for Germany. During the scherzo, electricity spontaneously rushed through the Visitor's body and out the crown of her skull. Her flesh was singing. It said Yes, yes, yes!

NAZI SEX CLUB

Everyone needs a little Nazi sex in their lives, Schatzi. That's our specialty, and we don't lack for customers. We're not in the guidebooks, but whoever wants to find us can do so without much bother. My sister and I have run this place since Papa died. After the Nazis shut down the Weimar sex clubs, they opened a few of their own. Papa ran the most notorious one right here in Berlin. It catered to industrialists, diplomats, celebrities, all the while spying on them and reporting their exploits to headquarters. In those days the audiences used to shout "Heil Hitler!" at the moment of climax.

After the war, Papa opened his own secret nightclub. Though he tried to shelter Jutta and me from the business, it's kept us clothed and fed these last forty years. Now we're the same age as

Papa was when he died from his heart attack. It's not logical, I know, but Jutta and I half-expected to go like him—at the club, chasing a troublemaker off the stage. Influenza took our mother when we were infants. You can't miss what you never had, Schatzi. Our biggest challenge? We have many. But keeping the old Nazi uniforms intact is number one. You see, Jutta and I are sticklers for authenticity. We don't stoop to cheap imitations, like our competitor. Ja, there's a similar club on the other side of Berlin, but it isn't as professional, as *meticulous*, as ours.

My sister and I were born in '47. We grew up in the wake of the war's suffocating fog. Our agenda? Bitte, we have no agenda other than defending people's rights to their memories, their histories, their fantasies. It doesn't matter what's true, Schatzi, if it's true for them. What I can assure you is that there's no end to the longing, or to the loss. And for the record, we're *not* Nazis. Smokers and drinkers, like our father, yes; stout like him, too. But not Nazis. Sure, Himmler's daughter was a regular some years ago, but she came more for the live jazz than anything. Members of her Stille Hilfe frequented our club, too, though we did not support the group financially, or in any other way.

Our sex shows? They're live, six nights a week.

Our actors are among the best in Germany. Many have careers in the adult film industry, here and abroad. It's our policy not to use smoke or mirrors or distorting lights, though we've taken extensive measures to ensure that our nightclub is soundproof. As you might imagine, privacy is a top priority for our clients. We enhance our performances with slideshows of Nazis at the height of their powers—uniforms impeccable, medals gleaming. No photos of bombed-out Berlin here. No poverty, or desperation. No Trümmerfrauen shoveling the rubble from the streets. Our plot lines are variations on a single theme: the intoxication of power, or rather, its imbalances.

Offensive, you say? Of course, you're entitled to your opinion, Schatzi. But what we offer is of utmost significance to our patrons. I might add that they come from around the world for our shows. The Japanese are particularly fond of our club. Like us, they were humiliated after the war. Like it or not, the Reich is a crucial part of our legacy. Instead of shunning it, Jutta and I make it accessible to those in need. For even outcasts have their needs, nicht wahr? I'd venture to say that our services have prevented a fair amount of hooliganism in Berlin, and beyond. My sister and I believe that when you can safely indulge your fantasies, you're less likely to act on them in real life.

Ja genau, we get our share of disturbed customers but probably no more than other establishments. Our bodyguard, the ever-loyal Otto, handles the nuisances. I suppose you could say the range of reactions is predictable. At their most agitated, our patrons cry out with rekindled—or even borrowed—memories. A few of the very oldest nurture nostalgia for their once-privileged positions in the Reich, golden times when they'd lived, briefly, as gods. At our club, they get to relive those days without judgment. True, they can get rather imperious, but it's nothing we haven't grown accustomed to handling. You know, Schatzi, so many of our regulars were dying in the eighties that I feared we'd go out of business. But after the Wall came down, a flood of East Germans picked up the slack. That's right, the Ossis weren't denazified like us in the West.

Since the fall of the former Soviet Union, we've gotten a steady stream of Russians demanding their own reenactments. For them, we offer Russian Night once a month—and the club is always packed. Our Fall of Berlin Supper Show is a big hit. We make the experience as realistic as possible by serving army rations (our chef has done his homework on that score) and playing a recording of Shostakovich's Leningrad Symphony on a continuous loop, interspersed with a soundtrack of Katyusha rocket launchers. We reenact the assault on German women, too. Ach, there's always a fuss, girls screaming, the Ivans shouting to go after this one or that. Typical of the times. War is hardly a pleasant affair, I agree, yet these evenings are festive. And the vodka flows freely.

Stimmt, Jutta and I live by ourselves. This work is time-consuming, frequently exhausting. To relax we enjoy playing Scrabble. Jutta is a fierce competitor and wins almost every game. She's begun entering local tournaments. Nothing like a good compound noun to bring her an avalanche of points. But honestly, Schatzi, this matters a great deal more to her than it does to me. In the afternoons, we have our coffee here at Café Wintergarten. I agree, they have a lovely Erdbeerkuchen, though my favorite is their poppy seed cake. Have you tried it? And the little bookstore downstairs is quite well stocked, don't you think?

I'm pleased we've met, too. You must join us for coffee again while you're in Berlin. It would be our pleasure, truly. As our dear departed father used to say: *Life is only as good as you decide it will be.*

Djazia Alves
EYE DOCTOR

1.

In her dream, she is nameless. She has no parents, no guilt or joy or grief. Nothing she's done seems to matter. Not her medical degree, or the hundreds of cataracts she's replaced. Not the people she's saved from blindness. It might be autumn, or winter, or spring. The skies reveal nothing. She drifts through the last hour of night before rising to go to the hospital. A thread of saliva, spider fine, clings to her chin. O meu país, she whispers.

The wind ushers her back to her girlhood in Luanda, to the distant singing of market vendors: Coconuts! Cassava! Maracujá! Pé de moleques! These last are her favorite—nut caramels so sweet they make her mouth water. Lizards scamper in the leaves. Eyes are watching her from the edge of the forest. Soon she must take up her microscopes again, her colibri forceps, her Keratome blades. Without their exactitudes, her mistakes would be too great.

2.

Djazia Alves shakes off her dream and lies in bed, listening to the morning rain. Since her pregnancy she's been dreaming profusely, as if her unborn were conjuring images for its own entertainment. Djazia considers this child, a mere four months in production. Already it's consuming her, feeding off her flesh, scalding the convex walls of her belly. The father, an Italian retinal specialist, was a hookup at the ophthalmology conference in London. She's told him nothing of the baby's existence.

Djazia tries on swaggering baptismal names: Anastasia, Hélène, Bonaparte. She imagines the child absorbing their rhythmic welter. Fleetingly, she'd thought of abortion, but she is nearing middle age and another pregnancy is unlikely. Djazia herself was born of her mother's passing romance with a Cuban soldier who'd fought in the Angolan Civil War. Ephraim Cabrera had walked to Luanda after long months in the bush. Angular and copper-colored, he asked Mãe for a drink of water while she was on schoolyard duty. She pointed to the outdoor spigot. When he drank his fill, she said, "Wait here, Soldier. I'll help you when the day is done."

But it was his gratitude—understated, sincere—that seduced Mãe. He wasn't insolent like the city men she knew, strutting around like roosters with two combs. Right then, she decided to take the soldier home. Mãe invited him to bathe in her tin washtub, offered him a bowl of her leftover yam stew, coaxed him to rest under the shade of the silk cotton tree. What came next surprised them both: "I'm a virgin," she announced as boldly as she'd exhorted her students to memorize the battles of the Napoleonic Wars.

Djazia was her father's replica—long limbed and graceful, her lips embarrassingly full. This was the curse of her girlhood. How gladly she would've traded her beauty for the love she saw in other mothers' eyes. But no matter Mãe's prayers to a pantheon of gods, her Cuban lover never returned.

Once, Djazia saw a photograph of Havana in an old propaganda pamphlet, its curve of coastline even more breathtaking than northern Angola's. She imagined her father taking her to Cuba, away from her brooding, violent mother, to a place she could sleep without fear. Before Djazia was eight, Mãe had tried to kill her three times: first, by stuffing an oil-soaked rag down her throat; next, by abandoning her in the jungle; lastly, with three slashes from a blunt machete. Nobody believed Djazia, not even when she showed the scars on her stomach to the parish priest.

Djazia is often struck by the ease with which others experience happiness. In the Guatemalan highlands, where she volunteered to do cataract surgery last year, an Ixil elder stared into her eyes as she examined his. "Offer your sorrows to the trees, Little Sister," he said. "They are generous and will absorb your sorrows."

But what are her sorrows exactly? That she'd longed for a mother's love? Longed for it when Mãe ran off with a German iron-ore dealer and reluctantly sent for her eight months later? Munich was frightening—crowded, deafening, the cars alarmingly fast. The new language hurt her throat, as did the Germans' rudeness, their insistence on her not belonging. To them, she was either invisible or hyper visible, nothing in-between. At school Djazia's classmates taunted her, except for Yonca, the shy Turkish girl who was a genius at math.

When her mother's affair with the German ended predictably—in the streets with Mãe and their belongings in shopping bags—Djazia helped her clean the shiny homes of the rich to survive. An exceptional student, Djazia left home at seventeen to attend university in Berlin. Mãe told her daughter that from then on, she was on her own. *Nothing but bad luck you've brought me!*

Djazia burned memories of her mother on an imaginary pyre, pictured the smoke rising past the tallest poplars to the vanishing clouds. Recently, she learned that her mother was on her deathbed back in Luanda. It's irrational, Djazia knows, but she fears that her mother—blind and clawing and breathing her last—could drag her headlong toward the diminishing light.

Bitch. Mãe de merda. Let her die alone.

3.

It's the most mundane of procedures, mechanical, really. Djazia could teach a motivated teenager to do cataract surgery in four or five months. Today, she's operating on Frau Wildgrube. Last year, under local anesthesia with intravenous sedation to remove an anterior orbital tumor, Frau Wildgrube rambled on about the war. She'd been fourteen when the Soviets marched into Berlin. *The Ivans hunted us down like animals. We disguised ourselves as boys, smeared feces in our hair . . .*

Djazia makes two incisions in Frau Wildgrube's left eye. Her steady hands are why the Germans couldn't kick her out of training. They tried one pretext after another: her "inadequate" early education in Angola; her "proclivity for tardiness" (once arriving two minutes late to grand rounds); her "brusque" manner dealing with superiors. To penetrate the upper echelons of medicine, she learned, you had to be one of them.

After emulsifying the cataract, Djazia vacuums it out. The patient's iris is floppy and the pupil constricted. Djazia inserts a

Malyugin ring to dilate it. Without warning, Frau Wildgrube re-
sumes talk of the war. *One soldier brought me eggs and cheese to fatten me
up, promised me cream and chicken if I returned with him to Leningrad.
I felt guilty eating more than the others, but they didn't have to pay with
their flesh like I did.* Frau Wildgrube's legs stiffen; her jaw clenches.

"We're nearly done. You were an excellent patient," Djazia re-
assures the old woman, a former lawyer. How worn-out her voice
is from everything she can't say. She injects the new lens into the
capsular bag, where it unfolds in a flash of light. Djazia's own eyes
remain her best weapons. They can stop even the most ill-mannered
idiot with a glare. Frau Wildgrube flinches as Djazia administers
the anti-inflammatory drops. Twice a month, she visits a nursing
home on Karl-Marx-Allee to care for patients, mostly women, who
are too weak to come to her office. How many, she wonders, have
suffered like Frau Wildgrube?

An orderly wheels Frau Wildgrube out of the operating room.
Her godson waits for her in recovery. He looks like a pensioner.
Berlin is a city of pensioners, pensioners and artists. Djazia removes
her surgical mask. This is her final case of the day. She steps out
on the hospital balcony, rolls a cigarette, and sits wide-legged on a
concrete banquette. Next week, if all goes well, she'll remove the
cataract in Frau Wildgrube's right eye. Then the old woman will
see perfectly.

LITTLE GOLDFISH

What are the odds of finding him in this asylum, though neither one of us is insane? And don't think that just because I, like Oskar Matzerath, am short-statured that we're carrying on like rabbits. Do you assume that two full-statured people would be fraternizing on the basis of vertical compatibility alone? For the record, my father was six foot three to my mother's five feet, and they were the rare happy couple, may they rest in peace. Nine years ago they died in a car wreck on the Berliner Ring. Social services didn't know what to do with me, a mature, two-foot-ten-inch woman with excellent knitting skills. And so they placed me here.

Everyone was eager to match me up with Herr Oskar. He's something of a celebrity and a relative giant at four foot one—a height difference, please note, identical to that of my parents. How old is he? Why, he might be a hundred for all I know! His orderly, the taciturn Bruno, listens to Herr Oskar's stories all day long and responds with tangled sculptures of string. I heard these very same stories but didn't believe a word of them. "Liar!" I accused Herr Oskar more than once. This amused, rather than annoyed, him. But soon I, too, fell under his spell. Here, have a look. I've crocheted these doilies in the bright reds and whites of Herr Oskar's battered tin drums. That's very kind of you to say, Dear Visitor. Vielen Dank.

No, I'm not especially attracted to him, though who can deny his boyish appeal? Despite the reputedly magical qualities of his hump and Bruno's assurances regarding Herr Oskar's manhood, I remain hesitant. My true objection? Let me just say that Herr Oskar's taste in women runs to the, eh, tawdry: telephone operators, slatternly housewives, nurses in their starched uniforms. Call me old-fashioned, but I require a certain courtliness in my suitors: flowers (preferably gardenias), chocolates (with hazelnuts, danke), freshwater pearls (a promising start). Frankly, Herr Okar's indifference regarding romance leaves me cold. Only last week, he took up with a lachrymose incurable from Bavaria. Genau, that shapeless cream puff! But this is none of my concern, Dear Visitor, nor should it be of yours.

Ach, listen to the old boy now: Herr Oskar is recounting the tragic tale of how his mother fell mortally ill after gorging on her cuckolded husband's eel soup—eels which he'd harvested from the sea with a dead horse's head for bait. Liebe mich, every time he gets to the part where the eels slither out of the rotting horse's eye sockets, I turn positively green. I suspect that his mother was the only woman Herr Oskar ever truly loved. Sicher. That is often the case with Lotharios. Now and then he mentions a dead sweetheart named Roswitha. Herr Oskar swears he still speaks with her ghost. Dear Visitor, what do I care if what he says is true? I insist only that it be compelling. From him I've learned that for the truth to blossom, lies are necessary.

After Bruno departs in the evenings, Herr Oskar and I settle in to play Skat until the wee hours. It's a nostalgic game for him, reminding him of his modest role in the defense of the Gdańsk post office during World War II. Lately, though, I've been teaching him to play Texas Hold'em. It's what the professionals play at the World Series of Poker in Las Vegas. How my palms itch to compete with the big boys there! Surely they'd underestimate me, but that is part of the allure. I've thought through my plan. I can see it all so vividly, down to my alias: Little Goldfish. I'd wear wraparound sunglasses, a sequined evening gown, and bring along a gilded booster seat. Na ja, they might laugh at me at first—that is, until I wipe the floor with their arrogant grins.

Herr Oskar encourages my dreams. "Fiat lux," he whispers to me at bedtime, gently rolling his drumsticks against his latest tin drum.

"Fiat lux," I whisper back.

THE CAPTAIN

I like my causes lost.

—VOLKER BRAUN

Few of us wake up anticipating the day that we'll die. And so it was for the 2,117 passengers on the maiden voyage of the SS *Zufrie-denheit*, the most lavish of the KdF ("Strength through Joy") cruises. These vacations at sea, subsidized by the Reich for working-class families, were designed to solidify the Volk's allegiance to the Führer and induce in them a willingness to sacrifice everything for the Fatherland. Onboard, every last man was a Nazi.

I was the captain of this dubious pleasure ship. Until that point, I'd succeeded in avoiding protracted associations with the Party, thanks to family connections. My childhood was a priv-ileged one: summer horseback riding on our Prussian estates; long winter nights reading by the fireside. My father, Konrad von Thorn, disapproved of the Russian authors I revered (Dostoevsky,

Tolstoy, Chekhov), blaming them for my rebelliousness. At nineteen, I publicly renounced the Lutheran church and took up with a married woman of lower class, mortifying my family. To avoid further scandal, Father forcibly enlisted me in the Kriegsmarine as the Second World War loomed.

On the morning a Soviet submarine torpedoed the SS *Zufriedenheit*, a strange dream awoke me before dawn. In my dream I was a boy at the village Konditorei, demanding to sample the hazelnut torte. The baker refused me with a curse. I stormed off, indignant at his insolence and vowing revenge. In that bleary moment, I forgot that I was captaining a ship packed with Nazi vacationers. Outside my porthole, a narrow scrap of moon peeked through the fog. I donned my dress uniform, ordinarily saved for ceremonial occasions, and toured the decks, encountering only a wraith of a woman walking three dachshunds in knitted vests.

When the torpedo hit our bow, it jolted awake every last person onboard. In an instant, I knew that our hull was irreparably damaged. It would be a matter of hours before the SS *Zufriedenheit* would sink into the frigid waters of the Baltic Sea. I envisioned the crucible to come: decks slippery with wailing passengers, their lives extinguished or changed irrevocably; and my name, the name of my illustrious forefathers, forever linked to this disaster. I vowed to behave honorably as captain of my ship. No matter the dire circumstances, I refused to let it sink without saving whomever I could.

As you might imagine, passengers died in great numbers, frequently trampling one another onto the lifeboats, which collapsed into the sea amid the mayhem. The Nazis alternately cursed God and beseeched him for mercy in every German dialect. Mothers clung to their children as the waves swallowed their last breaths. Above us a flock of cormorants circled soundlessly in the phosphorescent fog, as if keeping vigil.

In the last frantic hour, I married nine couples (my prerogative as ship's captain), two of whose members were wed to others onboard. The most touching was a pair of wide-eyed youngsters in love. They looked like siblings—tenderly squat, their thick fingers interlaced. Yes, Dear Visitor, I married them, too, before they raced below deck to consummate their union. Other passengers demanded divorces, though I wasn't licensed to perform those. I held fast to the no-divorce rule, even when one desperado threatened me with his pistol (luckily for me, it jammed).

Who survived? Some 312 passengers, the majority of them men and, disproportionately, Nazi leaders. In a crisis, the most selfish prevail. The worst of the bunch became policemen after the war. I've often thought it shameful that I survived alongside these thugs, who publicly cursed the "subhuman" Russians for the sinking. Several even had the gall to suggest that their own unwavering faith in God and the Party had spared them from drowning. Not a word about the savage shoving and shooting of those who got in their way. Nor of the final, pitiless silence.

To be plagued with memories is one thing, but it is quite another to relive them aloud. My dear, it's probably best to leave history well enough alone. To remember too much unsettles one's stability, devouring the present and what little remains of the future.

What was I thinking as I faced the end, you ask? The divinity of God? The prospect of heaven? No, Dear Visitor, none of these. Perhaps it's indelicate of me to say, but the truth is that I thought, rapturously, of Magda Grawert's breasts. Yes, she was the married woman with whom I'd scandalously consorted as a young man. In what I believed to be my final hour, I recalled Magda's breasts— pale, lovely, quivering, sad. Like this heartbreaking spring day.

Dagmar Trapp

DOPPELGÄNGER

Is not your dream
to be one day invisible?

—RAINER MARIA RILKE

It never happens anymore, Gott sei dank, but it lasted a good twenty years. When Eva Braun killed herself, I was just another starving twelve-year-old on the outskirts of Berlin. For a long time very few people knew who Eva was, who she'd *become* before dying alongside the Führer, his bunker bride of forty hours. After the war, photographs of the two of them surfaced, many taken by her— she'd started out as a photographer, you know—and Eva became a national obsession. By the fifties, we knew everything there was to know about her. As it happened, Liebe, I came to resemble her to an astonishing degree.

Wild speculations began to circulate that Eva was still alive. That she'd been spotted at the farmers' market in Lichtenberg (my hometown). That she was working as a shop girl at KaDeWe, selling French perfume (that was me). That she'd changed her name to Trudi Stern and was appearing onstage in Berlin's theatrical fringe (that, too, for a brief time, was me). Eva's shadow followed me everywhere. Though we were nearly identical physically, I cultivated other resemblances: arranging my hair like hers, practicing her Führer-adoring gaze, even adopting two Scottish terriers, her preferred pets. I walked mine daily in the Tiergarten, in part—I admit it—to hear the gaping passersby whispering: *Could it be her?*

There's no worse celebrity than being mistaken for somebody else; worse still when that somebody is a celebrity by association, not by her own achievement. So, to answer your question: Yes, I became notorious, but meaninglessly so and twice removed. It's difficult not to sound melodramatic, but I blame my likeness to Eva for ruining my youth. By the time I was thirty-three—the age my doppelgänger cracked that cyanide vial between her pretty teeth—I'd divorced three husbands and suffered multiple suitors, all of whom were wracked with distorted longing for *her.*

My third husband, Gerwald, was a biscuit manufacturer who used to blow kisses at me like a schoolboy. But he, like the others, was too terrified to touch me. For our wedding night he'd had a special altar built on which he instructed me to lie naked, motionless as a corpse, and strewn with rose petals. Then Gerwald lit a halo of candles around my head, muttering Hail Marys and gazing at me for hours. Fortunately, our divorce settlement left me financially comfortable enough to purchase this Charlottenburg flat. I'm right around the corner from all the lovely antique shops on Suarezstraße. You know, I'm quite susceptible to knick-knacks—I can't help myself.

Anyway, after the disaster of my last marriage, I put a stop to the Eva charade by dyeing my hair black and penciling on a facial mole. Then I promptly gained ten kilos by gorging on cured meats and hazelnuts. It was a relief, finally, to be invisible. I returned to my job selling perfume at KaDeWe, where I remained until I retired sixteen years ago. You know, I broke every sales record for my French company and was twice awarded vacations in Paris.

My dear, let's not enclose ourselves indoors today. The lilacs are in bloom, and the acacias nearly so. Soon my life will be over, but you're still a young woman. Do you have a husband? No? Why, fifty-four is the prime of life! Just wait until you reach my age. We may wish to avert our eyes from decay, but it's our natural state. After all, what is more ravaging than time? In truth, my own life feels no longer than this languorous spring day. Tell me, how is that possible?

Most mornings I stroll the grounds of the Charlottenburg Palace as I once did the Tiergarten. Its faded grandeur reminds me that everyone and everything, however sublime, must pass.

María Elena Molina

REICHSTAG

Dr. Molina: Do you know what the eighth wonder of the world is?

The Visitor: No, what?

Dr. Molina: Un cubano que no hable mierda.

Even for an academic specializing in modern Europe, it was a complicated story, or at least it grew more complicated than she expected. Dr. Molina was in Berlin doing research on the Blue Division of the German SS, which had been comprised largely of Spanish soldiers. While poring over archival military records, she discovered that her maternal grandfather had fought among them. The citation noted that one Alfredo Molina García of Zaragoza had been decorated by the Blue Division for singlehandedly disabling a T-34 tank near the Brandenburg Gate and killing seven Red Army soldiers of both sexes.

This was a radically different story than she'd heard growing up in Hialeah, in the heart of the Cuban exile community. Her family had toasted Abuelo Alfredo's war heroism without fail at birthday parties, christenings, Noche Buenas. Every New Year's Eve, when they counted the grapes, threw a bucket of water out the window, and shouted "Next Year in Havana!" her grandfather's exploits would be loudly extolled. Dr. Molina assumed this meant that he'd fought with the Allies, but nobody bothered to correct her. She tried to imagine how a man of his convictions might've reacted to such a distortion of his legacy.

Dr. Molina provided the Visitor with essential historical context. In 1941, she said, General Franco called for volunteers to help the Nazis fight Soviet Bolshevism, and forty-eight thousand Spaniards signed up in two days. Like her grandfather, many of the volunteers were former Falangists, who continued to wear their telltale blue shirts. Battle-hardened Fascists, they'd fought not only in Spain but also in Italy and North Africa before signing up with the Nazis to fight the Russians. These mercenaries were credited with taking Stalingrad—and holding the city, against all odds—for the Germans, at least for a time.

As the tide of the war turned, Franco recalled his men, but almost none withdrew. A hardcore group (along with some French SS) stayed on long enough to defend the Reichstag. On the day Berlin fell to the Red Army, the Spaniards knew they were dead men and fought to the bitter end—mano a mano, stairwell to stairwell, with grenades, knives, everything they had. Dr. Molina assumed that since her grandfather had made it as far as Berlin with the remnants of the Blue Division, he, too, must've perished in the Reichstag.

In the basement where the worst of the fighting took place, the historian slid her hands over the old bullet holes in the pillars and walls. She translated the faded Russian graffiti for the Visitor— victory slogans and florid curses, she explained, which had made

Gorbachev laugh out loud on a visit some years ago. Dr. Molina said she's tried to picture her Abuelo Alfredo—eyes wildly bulging, bearded, stinking, determined—battling his Bolshevik enemies to the last. He was forty-two when he disappeared.

"The upheavals of history," Dr. Molina told the Visitor, "create the most improbable of human consequences."

Her grandfather, she continued, was survived by his wife, Raquel, and their three daughters, the youngest of whom was the historian's mother. In 1947, when Alfredo Molina still hadn't returned from the war, his wife agreed to marry Diego Mosqueda, an ambitious tradesman who immigrated with her and the girls to Havana. Dr. Molina's mother became 100 percent Cuban and, at seventeen, eloped with a young revolutionary who died fighting with Fidel Castro in the Sierra Maestra. ("What is it about these women and their politically extreme soldiers?" Dr. Molina asked.) The mother subsequently fled to Miami, where she worked as a maid at a beach resort. Eventually, she met her husband—also a Molina—who, after waiting tables, fixing cockfights, and trafficking in illegal rhino horns (for their purported aphrodisiacal properties), became the air-conditioning king of Hialeah.

According to Dr. Molina, her grandmother kept a worn photograph of her first husband in her nightstand drawer. The historian showed it to the Visitor. Alfredo Molina wore civilian clothes, and his right hand rested on a holstered pistol at his hip. His eyes seemed to emerge from his temples, giving him a vaguely amphibian air. On the short side and ostentatiously muscled, he was nevertheless an attractive man. It was said he'd had to shave twice a day to control his stubble. Alfredo Molina had tried factory work, farming, and shoemaking, all unsuccessfully. In the end, only soldiering had suited him.

Dr. Molina pointed to the self-satisfaction in her grandfather's expression, "as if he knew his missions were holy." Her grandmother, the historian said, often tucked this same photo into her brassiere for comfort, or held it pressed to her ear for advice. *Do you hear him, María Elena? Do you hear him?* Abuela Raquel used to murmur, fluttering her husband's black-and-white face close to her granddaughter's. *Sí, Abuela*, she always lied.

"Cubans," Dr. Molina said with a shrug, "frequently have trouble distinguishing the living from the dead."

Anonymous
TANGO

It's your birthday, Hilde. I know this because everyone congratulates you. You're popular here, yet you remain aloof. Taller than everyone but exceedingly feminine, too, with a snug red dress that flares at the knees. Your legs are long, your hips child-bearing wide. I can only imagine your scent. It's my first time at this gathering by the Spree River. It's a dazzling afternoon in June, the weather so perfect it banishes memories of February. Along the river, tour boats play their recorded histories. Tourists stop to watch the dancing, to take photographs with their monstrous lenses. Later, they'll show their friends back home: *Look at the queer tango dancers in Berlin!*

I'm dressed as an Argentine sailor, with a striped shirt and a beret. Women tell me I have a masculine grace, predatory eyes.

Today I hold my gaze for as long as it takes for you to notice me, to understand that you won't escape. *Hilde! Hilde!* Your friends call your name. Your hair gleams with every turn of your head. Others flirt with me, but I ignore them. I have a reputation in certain circles as a good dancer, a better lover. Nobody goes down like I do, though my fingers are more precise than my tongue. Would you want your eye doctor performing surgery with her tongue?

Most of the city's new architecture—dazzling, sleek—has sprung up along these riverbanks. Berlin longs to define itself by the future, yet it remains a hostage to its past. Who knows this better than us, liebe Hilde? Not long ago, we couldn't have danced in the open like this, legs intertwining, torsos twisting in sexy ochos. Do I detect a hint of grief in your eyes? Perhaps your family migrated from Poland and suffered, as many Poles have, for the better part of three centuries. Or did they hail from the Ukraine, another eternally suffering region, where cannibalism flared during Stalin's Great Famine? What was an orphan then but a child whose parents hadn't eaten her?

The cigarette burns close to my lips. Soon it will be time to make my move. You'll want to know my name. It's Anke Weitz. My profession? Forensic pathologist. Yesterday, I removed three golf balls from the stomach of a businessman fished out of the Kreuzberg canal. His life is over, but, for me, his story has just begun. *How did you learn to tango?* you'll certainly ask me. I completed my internship in Buenos Aires, I'll say, where a distant uncle had fled after the war. It was there, liebe Hilde, that tango took hold of me.

I'm guessing you're a librarian, a star among the city's dreary archivists. The zipper down your back glints in the sun. You wear velvety black, t-strap heels without a single scuffmark. They're new, and it appears you're breaking them in. Later, I'll remove those shoes, unsheathe the arches of your feet. Your toenails will be painted a hopeful pink. I'll kiss them one by one, the way your Oma used to kiss them when you were a child, counting backward from ten . . . vier, drei, zwei . . . You'll cry as you remember this. Then I'll soothe you with soft kisses, restore the piece of your heart your first girlfriend stole, she of the pierced labia and thigh-high boots.

The imported Malbec they're serving is acceptable, but the chicken empanadas are unforgivably bland. Most of the women here are accomplished professionals: lawyers or researchers like you, professors reexamining the past through a feminist lens. You'll find the latest in self-pleasuring devices on their nightstands. But you won't need yours, liebe Hilde. Tomorrow when you wake up after making love with me all night, you'll find it difficult to concentrate. For I am the woman who will disquiet your life.

Anything can happen on this humid day along the Spree. I might lose you from one moment to the next—lose that perfect poise, the press of your hand in mine. At last you grace me with your gaze, calm and inviting as the cloudless skies. An obvious visitor to Berlin—wearing sneakers, good God—asks you to dance. Short and mousy, she's an interloper, a curiosity seeker. She doesn't belong here with us. Startled, you settle into her arms. The visitor moves awkwardly, fumbles with the rudiments of tango's intricacies. You follow her as best you can.

You're compliant, Hilde, that is evident. You resist making decisions about your life. When the wave comes in, you ride it to shore—for the heat rising from your nipples, for the eddies of pleasure between your legs. Tango is an intimate conversation.

Ich hab an dich gedacht

Als der Tango Notturno

Zwischen abend und morgen

Aus der Ferne erklang

I have a recording of Pola Negri singing this in 1937. Ah, we will listen to it together, very soon. I run my thumbs along my suspenders, light another cigarette, blow smoke rings to the trees. They linger in the branches like miniature wreaths. I want to remember this moment, register this light, the ripe river scent mingling with the sweat of so many dancing dykes. Already, I could shape lumps of clay to the precise dimensions of your knees.

They say it's going to rain tonight, though the skies remain a two-dimensional blue. Come here. Closer. Now closer still. Listen to me: I promise to shield you from the storm, from the dust of your past, from those etchings of wolves in the volume of Grimm's fairy tales that frightened you as a child. But first, meine liebe Hilde: *May I have this dance?*

Tran Thi Bich

FLOWERS

The program in metallurgy was supposed to last five years. There was a demand for this knowledge in Vietnam. I was nineteen and would have done anything to get out of Saigon. All I had known of life was hunger and war: hunger during the war; hunger after the war. My father, two of my brothers, and six cousins sacrificed their lives in the fight. That kind of freedom has no meaning for me.

A high school teacher recommended me for the work-training abroad. Although I was first in my class in mathematics, I was denied entrance to the university. Why? Because my mother had been branded an enemy of the State for refusing to join the Communist Party. Those coveted university seats went to the children of loyal Party members, no matter how brainless.

I asked my mother: "Since when is logic a crime?"

"It has always been a crime," she said.

East Germany was on the other side of the world. They could have told me, *You are going to Mozambique*, and I would have gone just the same. My hope was to return to Vietnam a full-fledged engineer and rehabilitate my mother through my accomplishments. ("You took all my men!" Ma had screamed at Party officials. "I have nobody left to give!") She took to growing chrysanthemums in a scratch of dirt behind our hut.

In East Berlin, I was immediately put to work in a munitions factory and received the barest of stipends and food. They took 12 percent of my meager earnings. I lived with other foreign laborers in freezing barracks. Fraternizing with Germans was forbidden. I was one of only three women at the factory. The other workers viewed me as a China doll, a girl to dominate. Püppchen, they teased me, with a mixture of curiosity and scorn.

I befriended two Cubans on the assembly line. They were homesick, like me, an affliction I could not have imagined back home in Saigon. Osvaldo and Benito—black-skinned as the Angolans we worked with—professed their love for me. But I could not have returned to Vietnam with either one. If innocent war babies were shunned, their mothers treated like dirt, what would happen to me?

In the end, my boss raped me. It happened after the annual picnic, where everyone got drunk. Herr Stüber insisted on walking me to my barracks and then pushed me onto a corner cot. With one hand he clutched my throat and forced himself on me. There were no witnesses. Three months later, my condition became evident. I was given two choices: abort the baby, or face deportation. I had come for training, I decided, and would leave fully trained—or not at all.

During my second year in Berlin, the Wall came down. I did what other stranded foreigners did: applied for asylum and sold contraband cigarettes. Between this and selling fake Hong Kong diamonds, I earned enough money to eventually buy this kiosk at the Charlottenburg S-Bahn station. I am a fixture here now, like the announcer's voice, or the ground-floor bakery with its mediocre pumpernickel bread.

My customers know that my flowers are fresh-fresh—no next-day wiltings for them. Frau Trapp prefers my blue hydrangeas, though she always considers the pink. And Herr Willhaus buys two mixed bouquets every Friday—a bigger one for his mistress; the other for his wife. I slip a chrysanthemum in to each bouquet, to honor my mother. Today, it is Herr Willhaus's twentieth anniversary, and so he includes an embossed card with his wife's flowers.

"No extra charge," I say. "Schönes Wochenende."

"Danke!" he shouts as he climbs the stairs to meet his train.

Kaspar Seidel

AMNESIA

Show us your sun, but gradually.

—NELLY SACHS

I'm told my name is Kaspar Siedel and that I was once a well-known photojournalist. Last September when a Good Samaritan extracted me from the Spree River, I still had my (soggy) identification and clutched my ruined Hasselblad. Uncharacteristically, I was wearing a fine English suit. Of course, I remember none of this. During my lengthy stay at the hospital then at the asylum on the north edge of Berlin, my personal memories proved irrecoverable. Without a history, I grew to believe that my life was pointless; in a word, expendable.

When at last I was released to the custody of my sister, Henni, and her surly teenaged daughter, I felt no more kinship to them than to their screeching parakeets. Henni, a devout Catholic, remains convinced that my amnesia is willful. Her resentment toward me is inestimable. She believes I tried to kill myself, a mortal sin she appraises as unforgiveable. Her house abuts a church cemetery interred with illustrious Berliners. Their sarcophagi are in a shambles. Big enough to hide in, they are now chipped and desecrated with graffiti and swastikas. Yet it's here, among the dead, that I feel most at home. With my cheek pressed to a tombstone, I can ponder, undisturbed, the nature of time and our feeble attempts at marking its passage. For what can time mean to me, a man with no past?

Dear Visitor, the ghosts in Berlin aren't confined to cemeteries. Listen. Don't you hear their whisperings? Feel their tugs on your sleeves? Their stories lie beneath the stories that nobody wants to talk about. They haunt the present like palimpsests, shaping it with their hungers. Sometimes it takes an outsider—and I've become one—to see what we refuse to acknowledge: the secrets buried by shame, effrontery, intimidation, revenge. When one no longer belongs to a tribe—or is a newcomer, a visitor, like you—everything reveals itself. The patterns we miss through familiarity. The normalized horrors of the everyday. Dear Visitor, we learn our blindness as surely as we learn how to hold a spoon, or recite our childhood prayers.

By chance, have you heard the story of the lone trombonist? No? Well, he used to haunt the no-man's-land on the Western side of the Wall before it came down. Nobody ever saw him, but his listeners grew accustomed to his mournful, late-night serenades. When, inexplicably, he stopped playing, everyone missed the music.

■

In recent months I've been reviewing my archives, particularly the series I did on post-genocide Rwanda. I shuffle through the photos impassively, as I might a deck of cards: men without arms; women missing eyes and breasts; children broken by unspeakable loss. What words could possibly express their grief? My sister tells me that our parents died when we were teenagers, and that I have no children of my own. Photographs from before my "accident" show me heavier, my face bronzed by the sun. In one picture, I'm wearing a turban and smoking an enormous Cuban cigar. A stunning African woman, a head taller than me, stands at the edge of the frame. Above us, vultures cross-stitch the obliterating light.

My former agent, Werner Voigt, regales me with tales of our carousing on four continents. He informs me, rather gleefully, that I drank to excess (single malt scotch but I wasn't particular) and nurtured an on-again, off-again heroin addiction. My amnesia, it seems, has banished these afflictions. Former lovers—Katje, Renata, and the very pretty Steffi—have seduced me anew, believing their kisses will reawaken me like some slumbering prince. I've had to invent my ardor (not at all difficult with Steffi) in order not to disappoint them. Even so, the women agree in their complaints of me—diffidence, self-absorption—which, they contend, haven't changed one bit.

■

How do I spend my days? With my modest disabilities pension, I'm free to simply wander Berlin. The city is both strange and vaguely familiar to me. Perhaps I feel as you might—a foreigner struggling to make sense of a new metropolis. The maps I carry are only of superficial use, wouldn't you agree? For what can we discern of any place by its surfaces? Berlin's modern architecture is striking, forward-looking, intent on expunging its past. Have you been to the German Historical Museum, by any chance? Perhaps you are aware then that the city is essentially built on a marsh? Ja, richtig. Every sizable building project here requires professional divers to secure its foundations. You know what soothes me sometimes? Thinking: West Berlin no longer exists, so why should I?

What else might I offer you? Allow me to think for a moment. Nothing concretely useful, I'm afraid. Perhaps only this: that the greatest danger in life is certainty. Yes, I do believe that. Our last redoubt in the world is wonder. Wonder and *un*knowing. Now and then a random detail will stir me to faint recognitions: a row of dead beetles in the grass; the chapped knees of some dowager on the S-Bahn. Tantalizing signs reminding me that infinity billows out from every moment. That's when I lean in, sniff the air, cock my ears like a foxhound—and listen.

Theo Hass

ANTIQUES

Time is our enemy, Dear Visitor, yours and mine; even now, as I try to hold your attention for our first few minutes together. Who cares for real stories nowadays? Titillation? Yes. Melodrama? Natürlich. But a lifetime's regrets? Who wants to hear about that?

My biological mother was Cuban, but I have no idea whether she's dead or alive. I learned of her existence at my father's funeral, which also happened to be my twentieth birthday. A colleague of his, a medievalist by the name of Helmut Popp, blurted the truth before passing out from an excess of schnapps. Er hatte einen Affen, everyone said. When I shook him awake an hour later, Popp denied what he'd said and begged me not to trouble him again.

I harangued my poor mother—the one who raised me, that is—until she revealed everything that Father had made her swear to keep secret. That my birth mother was from Havana. That she'd come to East Berlin in the sixties to study agricultural engineering. That she'd taken a poetry seminar with my father and become pregnant by him. That one cold March night, when the snowdrops were in bloom, Mayda Acevedo surrendered her child (me) to her professor's wife and left Berlin without a trace.

Mutti cried as she told me the story. Her biggest regret was not my father's infidelity—after all, it had produced me, the love of her life—but that she'd been unable to conceive. For her, this was a tragedy, as she'd been raised with the mantra of Kinder, Küche, und Kirche, auch genannt die drei K. She, too, had been my father's student, a bright star who'd dropped out of college to become his third wife. In an ironic twist of fate, I grew to look like her—fair and big-boned, with the same pale, untidy mouth.

Ah, Dear Visitor, I'm overwhelming you with the disorders of too much history. May I bring you some tea and ginger cake? Nichts zu danken. By now, you must be wondering: *Well, then, who are you, Theo Hass?* Nobody special, I assure you. Middle-aged, as you can see. An amateur violist. I'd even venture to say something of a flâneur. There's nothing I love more than strolling the streets of this city. For me, the highlight of these summer weeks are the weekly lunchtime concerts at the Philharmonic. Yes, we must go together sometime.

Just yesterday, a delightful quartet—bandoneón, violin, piano, and a sublime bass clarinet—played modern tangos. In the north end of the foyer, a striking couple danced to the music, precisely yet with abandon. The woman was statuesque, with lithe, expressive legs. Her partner, upon closer inspection, was also a woman, dressed as an Argentine sailor. The two were mesmerizing, hallucinatory, more than equal to the music.

By all means, Dear Visitor, feel free to look around my shop. As you can see, I trade in silverware and curios from the Americas. War and revolution have offered me unparalleled commercial opportunities. Why deny it? I've made my living from others' misfortunes, collected the plunder of the dispossessed. In Cuba, as you know, everything is for sale: women, antiques, even the cultural "authenticity" missing in capitalist societies, our own displaced nostalgias. In the nineties, I imported vintage American automobiles from Havana—fantastic, big-finned Cadillacs, Plymouths, and an unforgettable '53 Studebaker Starlight Coupe that I sold for a fortune to a captain of industry in Düsseldorf. Na ja, that bit of business enabled me to buy this little shop on Suarezstraße.

You've been to Havana, of course? Then you already know that it's a city of braggarts and parasites, of exquisite illusions. It reflects back whatever a stranger needs. My first visit "home" was the most difficult. Suffice it to say that I spent a long, scorching summer *not* finding my mother. In the end, Cuban police had to escort me to the Miramar Psychiatric Hospital. Dear Visitor, nothing derails a man faster than unrequited love. For the whole month of September, I wandered the hospital's lavishly unkempt grounds, napped under its ceiba tree, and watched streams of cranes fly overhead. In the evenings, a schizophrenic hairdresser named Abelardo wrapped himself in bed sheets and sang boleros.

It was hurricane season, and I dreamt more than at any time in my life. One dream still replays like a broken record, un disco rayado—isn't that how you say it in Spanish? In the dream, I'm naked and have a young boy's body. I stand alone in a desolate field, digging a hole with a tarnished silver spade. My back is a sundial, registering the day's hot progress. The hole grows deep and its walls tower over me. When I'm done digging, I lie down on the cool dirt, grateful to rest. My muscles twitch with exhaustion, but the earth holds me in place, humming and soothing. It's always at that very moment that I wake up.

I've returned to Havana more than a dozen times since, praying like an altar boy for the miracle of my mother's appearance behind a gate, or sitting majestically on the crumbling seawall of the malecón. Over the years, a fair number of Cuban women, no doubt seeking financial gain, have claimed to be Mayda Acevedo. But not a single one ever convinced me that she'd studied in Berlin, or possessed what I imagined to be my mother's cool intelligence.

It's difficult to find bargains in Havana anymore. The great fire sale of the nineties is over. Yet somehow amid all this salvaged detritus—that silver serving spoon, these lorgnettes, those highball glasses from a long-forgotten party—I feel just a little closer to my mother.

III

WAR FUGUES

THE VISITOR

By June, most of Berlin's lilac blossoms were dead, but the bees still sought entry, secret passages to the sweet. The Visitor took to frequenting cemeteries, reading tombstones for portents, imagining the uplifted arms of the dead. Time here was sleepy, geological. She heard dry flutterings in the trees, lone syllables, whisperings she couldn't decipher. At times it seemed to her that the dead were more conversational than the living. Was she meant to escort a few of them to the page?

Berlin had risen from its own devastation, from Jahr Null—Year Zero—through feverish productivity and forgetting. Every day the Visitor walked by the end of worlds, stopping to read the Stolpersteine embedded in the city's sidewalks.

When she wasn't in cemeteries, she often went to museums and art exhibits. The Visitor studied Paul Klee's works at the Berggruen. His was a

peculiar genius of intricacy and color and erratic, anarchic patterns, each
painting a small exodus. The more Klee's scleroderma spread, strangling
his heart and lungs, the more radiance he produced. Thankfully, the dis-
ease spared his hands. Decades later, his last drawings would inspire the
tattoo that graced the hollow between her own daughter's shoulder blades.

    At the Hamburger Bahnhof, Martin Kippenberger was pulling the
wool over everyone's eyes with his posthumous exhibit. Amid the careful
nothingness, a museum guard sang in her best church voice: "This is pro-
paganda . . . you know, you know . . ." In another wing of the museum,
the Visitor stumbled upon the work of Swedish painter Hilma af Klint,
who'd created lush, mystical abstracts in the early 1900s, years before ab-
straction officially "began," years before its male practitioners were hailed
as geniuses.

    On the museum's café patio, a breeze ruffled the canal waters. Sparrows
plucked crumbs from the Visitor's Linzer torte. A standard poodle pranced
across the bridge. The summer heat was settling on the city like a damp
cloth. Buildings looked glazed, huge lozenges in the sun. The Visitor felt

increasingly scattered, as if she were losing parts of herself to others' memories. Who would collect all her pieces and reassemble her again? Feed her fears their daily slab of meat? The more the Visitor believed she understood, the less she noticed. Better to simply keep seeing, to hold her gaze. With any luck, understanding might come later.

The Visitor struggled with balancing what she found with what eluded her. On fortuitous days, stories dropped like gifts out of the windless skies, typically prompted by loneliness, or happenstance. Other stories—the forgotten, interstitial ones she'd come to Berlin to collect—she coaxed from the grist of history. Why was apocalypse so compelling? What did war keep offering that ensured its survival? At an old-age home off Karl-Marx-Allee, the Visitor spoke for hours with a desiccated ballerina who'd survived the fall of Berlin and later consorted with a Cuban dictator. A brilliantly plumed bird escaped the dancer's mouth, flightless for decades, eyes darting and desperate, only to die at her feet.

Berlin was altering the Visitor, carving out space for silence, hallucinations, distortions. Sundays were her hardest days. The families were out, picnicking in the parks, strolling down the fine avenues or along the Spree River. The Visitor was reminded of her own childhood, where none of that ever happened. To her mother, she was primarily free labor for the family restaurant. Even after the Visitor became a mother herself, Sunday was the day her own daughter went off with her father to the suburbs of Los Angeles for sushi and TV. If she could, she'd turn every Sunday to a Monday.

Self-pity was a costly distraction, and the Visitor tried to avoid it at all costs. Better to keep moving, to splash in the pool with the tough old Frauen in her water aerobics class. She was growing strong from all the walking and exercise. In fact, she was barely recognizable to herself— leaner and harder, inside and out. Who was that in the mirror? Her body wasn't done, not yet.

Dieter Fuchs

PREACHERS

Nobody knows my identity here. And if by some chance they learned it, they'd probably soon forget it. This nursing home is as obsolete as Karl-Marx-Allee over there—once the pride of East Berlin. My secret has little to do with East or West, and it predates my current misery by many decades. It's not my secret alone but one from the Reich's early years.

Tomorrow I turn one hundred. Ja, you heard that correctly. I was born in 1913 and have lived my whole life right here in Berlin. Except, of course, for those three summer months of 1935. That's when I went on special assignment to the United States on a false visa arranged by the Ministry of Propaganda. My mission? To study the oratorical styles of black preachers in the South. Precisely, Dear

Visitor. Even in Germany they were famous as masters of rhetoric, men who spellbound audiences with their electric "preachifying."

How did I come by the job? Quite by accident, I assure you. As a linguistic anthropologist working on my dissertation (I'm fluent in seven languages, including Russian, Polish, and Old Norse), I got tapped on the shoulder by one of my professors, a committed Nazi. He'd recommended me to the authorities, thinking he was doing me a favor. Naturally, I was flattered—young and stupid, I would say now—but it did lead me to the greatest adventure of my life.

After the briefest of preparations, I was sent off to the segregated South. The Great Depression was still entrenched in rural America, the people thin and in rags, their shacks barely weathering the mildest of rains. But the land was like none I'd ever seen, lush with strange hanging mosses and immense trees. And the dusk was alive with fireflies. I drove around in an old Nash roadster procured by my German contacts and presented myself as a student of the "Negro vernacular."

It was unprecedented for a white foreigner like me to take an interest in black churches, sermons, and ceremonies. It helped that my accent was pronounced, my eyeglasses thick, and that I gave away box after box of Butterplätzchen. I was a novelty at church socials and pie contests, for which I was recruited as an "impartial" judge. At one small-town bake-off, I awarded the top prize to a novice's sweet potato pie, to the vehement disgruntlement of the veterans.

That hot magical summer, I flattered the velvety-voiced men of the cloth and listened to their tales of Jesus bargaining for their souls. I accompanied them as they presided over baptisms, funerals, family disputes, and weddings, and I withstood a heat so fierce it often felt three-dimensional. I asked questions, took copious notes in my leather binder, and promised to profile the preachers in my "forthcoming book," which, needless to say, never materialized. To my surprise, most of them cooperated fully and permitted me to film and record them, on and off their pulpits.

"Tell it till your throat's on fire!" That's how the Reverend "Buddy" Fisk described his oratorical style. His hair, combed with brilliantine, smelled of coconuts, and he chewed mint leaves to mask his moonshine breath. Inside his clapboard Baptist church, his Georgia congregation urged him on: "Preach it, preacher, preach it!" Reverend Fisk was as passionate an orator as I'd ever heard— furioso, unfailingly inspiring. At times he pounded a fist into his palm, calling down the Lord to the modest assembly, or lowered his voice to a whisper so faint that the whole congregation had to lean forward to catch his words.

During one stifling Sunday Mass, when even the flies were barely stirring, I watched as a handsome woman—in a seersucker suit, she might've easily been mistaken for a man—collapsed in the aisle in her egg-yolk-colored dress and matching hat, shouting, "Praise be to God, I've found the Lord! O Jesus, sweet Jesus, one mo' sinner is acomin' home!" All the while, the choir sang:

If you cannot preach like Peter, if you cannot pray like Paul,
You can tell the love of Jesus and say, He died for all.

The Carolinas, north and south, were populated with an impressive number of fiery preachers. One of the best, Reverend Filmore P. Gaines of Chester County, cultivated—and freely distributed—what were reputed to be the hottest hot peppers in the known world, much hotter than the Scotch bonnets of Jamaica.

His parishioners credited his blistering homilies to these same peppers, and they bravely fried them in pork fat, or chopped them into their grits. One sampling had me facedown in the holy water. How his parishioners loved to boast: "Ain't nothin' hotter than the word of our Lord comin' out the mouth of Reverend Gaines."

Farther west in Alabama, I sweated through the endless sermons of another legendary preacher, the Reverend Cato Singleton, much beloved by his flock for his exceptional ability to exorcise demons, be the afflicted man or beast. He was credited with banishing Satan from the high school biology teacher and an unruly donkey on the very same Good Friday. Despite the Reverend's gifts, garden-variety sinners blamed their moral turpitude on his lukewarm brimstone.

■

Upon my return to Berlin that autumn, I submitted my research to the Nazi authorities. Quickly enough, I saw how the Führer and his inner circle incorporated the preachers' techniques into their own speeches to further hypnotize the German people. The rhetorical talents of decent religious men—their cadences and use of tremolo, their grand gesticulations, the call-and-response with their devoted flocks—were harnessed for the Reich's machinery. If only I could claim to have behaved courageously, or engaged in acts of sabotage, or attempted to withdraw my research from the Nazis. Instead I faded back into the woodwork of academia, kept to safe subjects (problems of linguistic relativity), and managed to survive the war by translating intercepted military communiqués from the Reich's many enemies (my extreme myopia saved me from conscription).

Years later when I met your Cuban writer friend, I knew the time had come to share my story. It was a relief to unburden myself. Dear A. kept me alive during the worst of the eighties, when the Eastern bloc went bankrupt. In his stylishly flared trousers and trench coat, he smuggled in an occasional bottle of rum, and he sustained me body and spirit. Once, he brought me a beautiful pair of oxfords from a Ku'damm shop. Though they pinched his feet, A. wore the shoes to East Berlin and exchanged them for my beat-up Polish loafers. Regretfully, I forced myself to scuff up the oxfords to avoid unwanted attention.

When will you be seeing A. again, Dear Visitor? I'm expecting him back in Berlin later this summer. Yes, with his wife. A charming woman, do you know her? Do please tell A. that I prefer dark chocolate to Havana Club these days. Ach, but I know him well enough. He'll insist that we go out for one last drink, always one last drink. And you know what I'll tell him? *Mañana, amigo, mañana.*

Frida Krechel

BREEDER OF GODS

Thank you for the tulips, my dear. So, we finally meet face-to-face. Won't you sit down? The audio book you sent inspired me, as I expect you knew it would. My eye doctor—she's an African, you know—says my glaucoma has grown worse. There's not much I can do except use these drops to lower the pressure. Here, I've made us some tea. Would you care for a slice of plum tart? I bought it fresh from the bakery downstairs. It's their specialty. Bitte, forgive my lack of ceremony, but if I don't begin right away, I'll lose my courage.

Richtig. As a child, I was told that my father had been a handsome Nazi officer and my mother a simple country girl. These were the standard lies. Intelligence wasn't important for the program, only racial purity. Much later, I learned that my grandparents had "volunteered" my mother as a breeder without her consent. Their reward? A cash bonus for their "sacrifice." The times were difficult, and a surprising number of parents surrendered their daughters for the program. It bestowed on the families a certain prestige, proof of patriotism, as if they were contributing to a top-secret mission.

A team of nurses raised us—yes, the breeding-program children. The nurses looked after our physical needs but deliberately withheld affection. They were specially chosen for this skill. Personal attachments were discouraged, as were emotional displays of any kind. Our devotions were to be channeled exclusively to the Fatherland. Despite the rules, attachments did form. We children comforted each other when we got sick, or skinned our knees, or cried for reasons we didn't understand. (Crying, too, was forbidden.) We formed our own families, though the word itself was banned.

The surface of our days were like other farm children's, I suppose. We milked the cows, shoveled out the barn, helped in the fields (harvesting barley, mostly). The girls were taught homemaking skills as well as basic reading and arithmetic. I learned subtraction by taking away "useless eaters" from productive citizens. Ordinary books, those with no "purpose," were strictly verboten. Instead we read texts designed to brainwash us into becoming fanatics of National Socialism. But what did we know about any of this at the time? Our reality was our reality, strange as it sounds now.

It's a miracle, under the circumstances, that I began questioning my upbringing. As an adolescent, the waters muddied for me. I challenged the nurses, refused their orders, their insistence on silence. Once, I escaped the farm during a lightning storm. When the nurses found me in a distant neighbor's chicken coop, they beat me to bleeding with a birch switch. Then they locked me up for three days in a storage shed without food. By law, they couldn't breed me until I turned eighteen. Pregnancy, they told me, would calm my temperament.

As the Reich's fortunes soared, the government funded other clandestine experiments. They kidnapped Aryan-looking children in Poland and Russia (after murdering their families) and transported them to Germany. Why? To increase the population and placate the barren women. There was nothing worse for a German woman in those days than to be childless. I heard that the Reich imported girls from Norway, too, more Aryan even than us.

The nurses kept control of us until the early spring of 1945. When defeat looked certain, they abandoned us. Those were frightening times, chaotic times, not knowing what would happen to us. We'd heard so much propaganda about the Russians that we feared their arrival as much as we did dying of hunger. When the war finally ended, we fended for ourselves as best we could, traveling in every direction, trying to find somewhere we might call home.

Oh, my dear, what *didn't* I do to survive? My upbringing ensured that I was unfit for any but the most menial tasks. For a time in Berlin I became a Straßenmädchen. But business was poor, even for a pretty girl like me. Why pay for a woman's favors when anyone could take what they wanted by force? Sometimes what must be said can't be said easily, or at all. I'd need something a lot stronger than this peach tea to tell you more. Let's just say there were women—starving, like myself—who offered themselves in exchange for food.

The following winter, I found protection with an American Negro soldier. One morning, he asked me what I most wanted in life. Do you know what I answered? *A sandwich thick with goose drippings.* That night, he brought me two. It wasn't love, not for me—I was incapable of that—but his kindness that kept us together.

When he invited me to move with him to Louisiana—he stood to inherit his grandparents' sugarcane farm—I declined. Six kids he wanted. But that was his dream, not mine.

Not long afterward, I met my husband at a pub where I was paid to flatter the clients into buying me watered-down drinks. Jan was a railway brakeman and twenty years my senior. I didn't ask him what he'd done during the war, and he never said a word about it. This was an unspoken agreement between us. Jan wasn't handsome, but he was gentle and asked little of me, and that was enough. No, we couldn't have children. One doctor told me that my insides looked like a war zone. Some breeder I turned out to be, eh?

Overall, I guess you could say I've been more satisfied than happy. I don't feel joy the way other people seem to experience it, yet I don't suffer as much either. It's hard to describe—a little like trying to sew closed an infinite hole. You see, my dear, the problem for me isn't enduring life's pain but its beauty. Ja, that's the harder, the much harder, thing.

SKIES

We were both Luftwaffe pilots, but we met in the boxing ring. Max S. was a famous fighter from before the war, a German hero. I was fifteen years his junior. We agreed to fight to amuse the other pilots, to help raise morale as our hopes for victory faded. Dear Visitor, how can I explain to you what it was like at the very start of the war, singing through the skies? The great dream of glory to which we were willing to lose our lives? On cloudless days, we watched the wings of our planes like birds of prey shadowing the land. We felt invincible.

Ja, that was before everything went to shit. Defeat, our superiors insisted, wasn't an option, and they pressured us to rat each other out. Every morning there were six new ways to commit treason. One kid from Hanover was hanged for telling a stupid joke about

Himmler. Ach, I don't remember how it went exactly—I'm useless at jokes—but it was a play on Himmel, or heaven. What does it matter? The point is that by then we were murdering our own faster than the Russians. On top of the world at eighteen; ruined and strung out on Pervitin at twenty-two. That's how it was then. We grew old, very old, before our time.

Sometimes I think it's better to remember nothing at all. Memories are selective. We pick and choose what we need to believe, what we require to survive. Have you heard about the guilt placards the Allies posted in town squares all over Germany? DIESE SCHANDTATEN: EURE SCHULD! (THESE SHAMEFUL DEEDS: YOUR FAULT!) They showed the very worst photographs from the camps. Everyone was shocked. This surprises you? How could we have known what was going on in every corner of the Reich?

Yet from the moment of defeat, we were determined to rebuild the country from zero. To carry on as if nothing had happened, as if millions of our own innocents hadn't been killed. We suffered our share of war crimes, too, but who could complain? Countries build weapons then need to use them, nicht wahr? That's the business of war. As for the pilots, who wanted to hear from us? We were living reminders of what everyone wanted to forget. Our self-respect vanished. Not a shred of it left. Don't get me wrong. I'm not saying our mission was honorable, only that there were honorable men serving it. We lost that honor. In the end, we were left alone to die in our pasts, hour by hour.

I worked odd jobs for a few years, on cleanup crews and construction projects. Anything for my daily bread. Ach, the tons of wreckage we cleared out! We found corpses trapped in the positions they'd died in, body parts gnawed to the bone by rats. Finally, I got lucky and landed a job selling men's shoes on the Ku'damm. It was a relief to escape the backbreaking work of banishing every last trace of the war from our midst. No matter what we accomplished, or how fast we accomplished it, the war lived on in our heads. Dear Visitor, there were times I was convinced I'd be better off dead. That I should've died young rather than live to endure such humiliation. But hunger shouts louder than dignity. Erst kommt das Fressen, dann die Moral.

Sure, I kept track of my famous opponent over the years. It was hard *not* to. Max S. lived to a ripe old age. When he turned one hundred, his birthday face was plastered on magazine covers everywhere. That day we fought in the ring? I knocked him out in the second round. Ohne Zweifel, he did very well for himself, very well. Grew rich working for the Americans—for Coca-Cola, in fact. Drove around Berlin in a gigantic Cadillac. The Yanks loved Max S. in that way they loved everything larger than life. In Germany, we were desperate for heroes, and so his war record was conveniently forgotten. His prowess in the ring was what everyone talked about. And later, his millions, his success. He was the great Max S., a national icon, the best part of who we needed ourselves to be.

Once, I fitted old Max with a pair of imported cordovans that cost more than two months of my wages. His feet were surprisingly narrow for so large a man. No, he didn't recognize me. Barely glanced at me, as I recall. He was too busy reading a newspaper article about himself. True, quite true. Anonymity can be a sobering mercy. In any case, he bought three pairs of those pricey cordovans and then disappeared in a cloud of cigar smoke.

Or perhaps, Dear Visitor, it was I who disappeared.

KIOSK

It's circumstantial, Schätzchen, like most things in life. There's no such thing as pure evil. As far as I'm concerned, people who make pronouncements about the innocent and the damned can't be trusted. I'm old now, half blind, nobody of historical interest. An ordinary person. Except for this: I've watched the whole world pass by my kiosk at the Hauptbahnhof. Trains coming and going, whistles blowing, countless tearful good-byes. The world is round and we keep moving and moving until we return exactly to where we started. Sag mal, what's the point of it all?

Sixty years I've been sitting here, first helping out Uncle Heinz, then taking over the business when he died. My uncle spent two years on the Eastern front and somehow lived to tell about it. All the rest of our family was killed in the air raids. I survived because

I stayed too long at the water pump flirting with a boy. When I ran home, everyone was gone—Mutti, my brother Franz (who'd lost both hands in Poland), and my baby sister Liesel. For weeks I wandered around Berlin, hiding in cellars and bombed-out buildings. I chopped off my hair, wore my brother's old pants, his falling-apart shoes. Skinny and flat-chested and with a too-big jaw, I passed for a boy. This saved me when the Russians came.

It was a miracle Uncle Heinz managed to find me at all. He asked around until someone directed him to a flooded bunker where a bunch of us street kids lived. He was in his forties by then—too old for the regular army but not for a police order battalion. Uncle Heinz went crazy from what he'd been forced to do. Crazy, meaning that he didn't hide the truth of what he'd lived. Everyone in the neighborhood was afraid of him. Too loose-lipped, they said. Dangerous. Wherever he went people held up their hands, as if trying to protect themselves. Our neighbor, Herr Drawert, threatened to kill him if he didn't *shut the fuck up.*

Why? Because for Uncle Heinz to own up to his crimes meant that everyone else might be forced to do the same. Und glaub mir, that was the last thing anyone wanted. Instead they shunned my uncle, treated him like a pariah. What people wanted most was to go about their business, rebuild their homes and their lives, polish their lies, and *not look back.* Everyone had at corpse in the basement, as the saying goes, but who would admit it?

After sixty years at this kiosk, Schätzchen, I can tell you that nothing is what it seems. Berlin isn't one city but many cities, and much bigger even than its myths. You've got to know where you're standing, what you're looking at. Like that old American car parked right outside the Hauptbahnhof. They say it used to belong to a famous boxer, someone you probably never heard of. The current owner keeps it parked there, gleaming and impeccable, as if his life depended on this. Shines it up himself on weekends with a chamois cloth. Who knows why people do the things they do?

I've seen every drama played out on these platforms—marriage proposals, heart attacks, jiltings, overdoses, suicides, and a shootout six years ago that left four people dead. Wieso? Who would read a book from the likes of me? Sehr lustig, Schätzchen. My plan? What a question! In the end, there's no ending. Me, I'm going to die on this very spot, waiting for the next whistle to blow.

Bettina Streim and Jochen Fick

HUNTERS

What was right yesterday, can't be wrong today.

—KLAUS FILBINGER, FORMER NAZI JUDGE

1.

There aren't too many of us doing this work anymore because there aren't too many of *them* left. Most are on their last legs, their minds gone, on oxygen tanks or dialysis machines. What has this career cost me? Everything, Dear Visitor, everything. My family. My friendships. My sleep. Isn't that enough? *Why do you go on, Bettina? Why have you spent your life interrogating these old Nazis? Haven't we paid a ransom in reparations already? They had to live with their crimes, no? Haven't we suffered enough?* And yet I persist with my investigations: *Isn't it true, Herr Krüger, Herr Scheer, Herr Grabitz, Herr Fick, Herr Bentheim, Herr Rohrbaugh, Herr Schlag . . . ?*

In recent years, we've been going after the Nazi "ladies" as well. Don't think for a minute that the fairer sex wasn't doing its fair share for the war effort. "Hitler's Furies," one historian called them. These women are living longer than their male counterparts, but their memories are equally selective. Why, they can't seem to remember if they were hunting rabbits or Jews in the woods. Or which drugs filled the hypodermic needles they used to "sedate" their patients. How did they acquire mink coats and diamonds on their salaries? Keine Ahnung. Yet when it comes to blaming others—*Those nasty Poles betrayed every last Jew they ever met!*—their memories fire up with astonishingly fine detail.

How many convictions have I secured? Dear Visitor, if I assessed the value of my work solely by the successes, I'd be too disheartened to continue. Please understand that we have only six lawyers on my team, each carefully trained to investigate war crimes. We've dedicated twenty-three years to rounding up the last Nazi criminals in our district. After this massive effort? How many? Fourteen convictions, three overturned on appeals, no sentence greater than eight years—and even those were commuted due to the defendants' failing health, or legal technicalities.

But what do the Nazis' lies matter to me anymore? What matters to me is continuing to shine a light on them. Flushing them out of their cozy hiding places, where they've been pretending for decades to be who they're not. Forcing them to squirm before their family and friends, before the unforgiving cameras. My dear, I don't give a damn how these murderers rationalize their lives. What spurs me on is justice—justice for the living, but especially for the dead.

2.

Who gave you my name? That bitch lawyer? She came after me for years and couldn't pin a fucking thing on me. That ball-breaker wasn't even born until ten years *after* the war. So, what's any of it to her? Sticking her nose in everyone's business—and for what? She made my life a living hell. Came after me like I was the Führer himself. My wife left me, my kids don't speak to me, and even the wrecks in this shit hole of a nursing home keep their distance, as if their own hands aren't stained with blood. How could *all* of them have been in the resistance during the war? Their lies, Liebchen, are as thin as your notepaper there.

Damn right, I took to drinking again. Who wouldn't drink shackled to that kind of stress? Nobody understands what we went through. Nobody. We were soldiers. We followed orders. We didn't have the luxury of sitting back with a fucking brandy and discussing the *moral implications* of every goddamn command. I killed a few people. Everyone did. There was a war on. I was an expert marksman. As a kid, I used to go hunting with my grandfather in the forests outside Berlin. No crime in a little hunting, is there? Just because I can do something doesn't mean I did it without justification.

I was a policeman for forty years after the war. Doesn't that count for anything? That bitch nearly got my pension suspended after I put my life on the line every day for the likes of her. Now I've got one foot in the grave, and they're still hounding me. *They're* the real criminals, if you ask me. Don't tell me you're ignorant about what the Russians did to us either. We didn't commit half the atrocities they did. They used their jeeps to pull apart our women like rag dolls. Raped them right in front of their own children. Nailed them to barn doors and crucified them. *Cruci-fied* them, do you hear me? Where's the big outcry about that? Fucking savages. We had to keep our mouths shut about a whole lot of other things, too. Like the thousands of Germans burned to death by the firebombs. That's right. They tried to wipe us out like an accursed species.

What the hell do you mean *that sounds familiar?*

Look, I don't have to talk to you. Who are you, anyway? Get out of my room. Nurse! Nurse! Get this woman out of here! She's agitating me! You know my heart's weak. I'm not going to sit and stand trial all over again. They had their day in court and they lost! Got it? They fucking lost!

Gabrielle von Holz

SWAN

Naturally, I was called upon to perform for the Führer on numerous occasions. I know what you're thinking: *Another collaborator beats her breast with disavowals!* My dear, I've no need of your sympathy. I had a choice—and I chose to survive. In fact, I bargained for my life every day. Nobody expected the slightest political intelligence from a ballerina, and so I insulated myself from the worst. I attended elegant soirées at the Hotel Adlon and danced cheek to cheek with those marionettes. Photographs of me appeared regularly in the press, including the *Völkischer Beobachter.* I performed on the stages of our allies in Italy and Spain, too, and in the conquered territories. The Parisians, in spite of themselves, gave me a standing ovation.

This rooftop solarium is one of my favorite places in Berlin. Here, even the octogenarians are naked. No matter the side-sliding breasts, areolas distended by time, the blue veins marbling bellies and thighs. Who gives a damn about any of it? We're alive, aren't we? And, deliciously, nudity is required in the Jacuzzi. Yes, *required*. No offense, my dear, but why are you still wearing that silly bathing suit? You say these sunbathers wouldn't be naked where you're from? A pity. Ach, the young are much too anxious in their beauty to remove their clothes.

I'm not sure why my background matters to you now. But if you insist, my dear, I came of age during the chaos and uncertainties of the Republic and the rise of National Socialism. For the record, my paternal uncle, a grandee military officer, was involved in the plot to assassinate Hitler. He was executed, of course, and our family estates in Silesia were confiscated and later subjected to Russian retaliations. Rich or poor, we were all left destitute. How could you possibly fathom the havoc and displacement near the end of the war? Hordes of starving refugees from the East arrived in Berlin every hour, crowding the railway stations, straining what was already beyond repair.

For me personally, the worst tragedy struck during one of the last air raids. I'd gone dancing at a nightclub near Wittenbergplatz. Natürlich, the clubs were open to the bitter end. How else could we have survived? A British waltz was playing—*Mrs. Miniver*, I remember this exactly. A chandelier fell, as if in slow motion, onto the crowded dance floor. Imagine for a moment the shattered glass, the panic, the sirens, the spattered blood. Days later, I woke up in the hospital with a crushed foot. And just like that, the war was over. With everything in shambles, I received scarce medical attention. Most of the doctors and nurses disappeared—to where, nobody knew.

I endured four operations over the next eighteen months, but these only exacerbated the limp that plagues me to this day. My dear, I suffered a depression so severe I considered throwing myself in the Spree River. Thousands of Germans committed suicide just after the war—survivors who'd lost loved ones in the bombings, women and girls gang-raped by Russian soldiers. I pictured river algae draping these girls' skulls, their sallow cheeks, the perch pecking at their lifeless eyes.

Implausibly, I reinvented myself as a modern dancer. Such was the disorder of the times and the grim mania to rebuild that even a crippled ballerina like me could succeed. Nearly overnight I became a symbol of postwar resilience, considerably more glamorous than those dreary Trümmerfrauen. Soon I was transfixing audiences throughout Europe with what one critic called my "choreography of the broken." Against power you play the politics of weakness, no? Nobody wanted to talk about the war, or the horrors we'd suffered. All hope lay in the future. But watching me dance permitted audiences a catharsis.

I assume you've seen clips of my performances? My limp was noticeable only when I wanted it to be, for dramatic effect. My costumes were a blinding white—a form of visual absolution—and I danced against a pitch-black backdrop. Very stark. Very startling. A deliberate amnesia. The music? Discordant, unpredictable, in keeping with the times. I danced my signature piece to Nielsen's clarinet concerto—a brooding, conflictual composition that mirrored the madness of the musician for whom it was written. Offstage, I treated my crushed foot with Chinese unguents and balms and drank enough gin to sleep soundly.

Only M., the American modernist dancer, was my equal in those days. She, too, performed to an advanced age, despite her arthritis. How we feared the ordinary like the plague! Both of us were obsessed with Greek myths and the idea of Jung's collective unconscious. Eagerly, we interpreted our dreams, submitted to lengthy psychoanalysis, and ate several apples daily for our health. During the war, I was in contact with a farmer who secretly supplied apples to me at steep prices, defying the Ablieferungspflicht.

In the fifties, despite our rivalry, M. and I premiered a piece at the Gran Teatro in Havana. You've heard about it? *Die Beiden Mädchen* was quite scandalous for its time. A pas de deux for women who danced, romantically, in a world without men. Ohne Frage, my dear, it *was* taboo-breaking. We performed at the behest of Fulgencio Batista, the Cuban dictator, with whom I had a memorable dalliance. He was quite taken with me, with the near transparency of my skin, and obsessively kissed what he called my pié de loto, my "lotus" foot.

The island's prima ballerina, though notorious for cold-shouldering her competitors, befriended M. and me. She invited us to her mansion at Varadero Beach, where we consorted with handsome, confident, *undamaged* men. Very unlike our German men, who were utterly destroyed by war—hopeless as partners, as men with power or pride (except the sick ones who carried on with their misplaced inflations). By necessity, many German women turned to our former enemies, and to each other, for comfort. After the extreme privations we suffered, who would dare judge us? Luckily for me, I had more options than most.

A husband? My dear, what possible use could I have had for a husband?

S. Benedikt Kohl
MISSING

Though it was summer, Benedikt Kohl was buttoned up in wool, as if he feared disappearing through an accidental gap in his suit. What he remembered most, he said, was the sense, as a little boy, of having been born to the wrong family. The smells were wrong. The games and lullabies were wrong. For a time, even German itself felt wrong on his tongue. But so thorough was his family's deceit that Benedikt mistrusted his own perceptions. The shadow life that haunted him, that mysteriously rose up in his dreams, had the air of a distant music, like an unseen bird in the woods. Gradually, this ghostly life receded, leaving only a persistent discontent.

Benedikt was raised in the Bavarian Alps, in a sleepy village whose men had been swallowed up by two wars. His father, Jürgen, was the barkeep of the sole pub, a man to whom everyone owed money or a favor, neither of which he insisted they repay. Nearly blind from a Great War injury, he discerned little more than shadows. Jürgen put his son to work in the pub at a tender age, serving beer and simple snacks. Customers treated Benedikt with a formal warmth, as if he existed behind glass. He reddened when they stared at him too long.

Benedikt's mother, resented by the villagers, was nonetheless civilly treated as Jürgen's wife. Martina was beautiful, much younger than Jürgen, and had won the dubious prize of becoming his bride. Two husbands by age twenty-six (she'd lost her first husband to a sniper in Czechoslovakia) was more than any local woman could've hoped for. But Martina behaved as if she were the unluckiest of them all. After Germany's defeat, the villagers gossiped about her new stockings and the foreign cigarettes she smoked in a tortoiseshell holder. As for her son, Benedikt, she mostly forgot he existed.

When Jürgen died of a brain embolism, Martina sold her husband's pub for a pittance and moved with Benedikt to Munich, where the world was converging for the purpose of reconstruction. She found work as a secretary to an American general with whom she became amorously involved. Tangible benefits resulted from their liaison: a requisitioned apartment, ample groceries (boxed cereals, bananas, canned cream of tomato soup), and a bilingual education for Benedikt. General Douglas Pitt had grown up in Chicago and spoke reverentially of the Cubs, its accursed baseball team, which narrowly missed winning the World Series in '45. He signed up a reluctant Benedikt for Little League as part of the Americans' denazification campaign of German youth.

It was at General Pitt's army base that Benedikt heard Russian for what he believed was the first time. It stirred him in a way he couldn't comprehend. Benedikt trailed the visiting Soviet officers to the dining hall, surprised that he understood a few of their phrases. *What's for dinner? The rations are better here. Chicken!* When he asked his mother about this, she responded by slapping his face. At university, Benedikt studied Russian history and language and completed his doctorate in record time. Few German students, understandably, were studying Russian then. Benedikt's early research focused on imperial Russia's nineteenth-century expansionist policies (he wrote two well-regarded books on the subject). And, in time, he became a history professor in West Berlin.

Before Benedikt's mother succumbed to emphysema, she'd enclosed a sealed letter to him as part of her will. In her childish hand and Bavarian dialect, Martina informed Benedikt that he was not, in fact, her biological son but a Russian orphan. As far as she knew, he'd been kidnapped somewhere on the Eastern front. About his origins, or the fate of his biological parents, Martina knew nothing; only that his name had been Sergei.

Benedikt reeled from the news. He embarked on extensive archival investigations and tracked down dozens of surviving orphans like himself. The resulting book, *Stolen Children*—a product of six years' furious work—was recently published to critical acclaim. For many orphans like him, the truth about their early lives finally made sense. During the course of his research Benedikt met his wife, Ottelie Kappel, a watercolorist who rendered dreamy, naïf recreations of her native Ukrainian village. Raised by a Methodist family in Münster, Ottelie suspected that her real parents had been Jewish. But neither she nor Benedikt had any living relatives whom they could question.

TRIO (CODA)

1

Ilse Schlusser

SACHSENHAUSEN

Most visitors come to Sachsenhausen to walk on the dead, to shake their heads and look down at us Germans. They're foreigners, like you—artists, historians, Holocaust tourists, a few Jews who dare to show up where their relatives perished. Those who survived the camp never return. As you know, my dear, not all the prisoners were Jews. There were gypsies and homosexuals, Communists, Russian soldiers—Stalin's own son died here—and others who ran afoul of the Reich. Even a famous Cuban transvestite known as "Silvia."

Stimmt. The camp did contract workers from the surrounding communities. These people grew potatoes for the prisoners' soup, delivered supplies, extracted gold from the dead Jews' teeth. Ordinary people, like my mother, neither brave nor evil, just trying to survive in difficult times. You mustn't forget that Mutti's generation grew up poor and humiliated after the Great War. *Without hope*, she used to say, *only the worst can happen.* Is it any wonder the Führer grew so popular?

Mutti was among the first guards hired here in 1936, and one of just a few women. At the time, she had no idea what Sachsenhausen would become. To her, it was a job—and it paid a decent wage, though a portion of her earnings went to compulsory dues and the Winterhilfswerk. She was tall, with a slim figure, and soon the Nazi officers were vying for her attentions. Of her many suitors, she chose my father because he alone promised to let her continue working after they married.

Things went well for them, at first. I was born in 1939, and my brother two years later. But as the war dragged on, my parents grew increasingly despondent. I remember my otherwise logical mother turning to an astrologer for advice and praying aloud that Goebbel's promise of a miracle weapon might be true. To imagine *not* winning, she said, was far worse than battling on. For her and millions of others, it was either fight or freeze to death in Siberia.

My dear, what kind of question is that? How could she have done things differently? You can't escape the times you live in! As the Russians marched on Berlin, it was my father who swallowed the cyanide. Other officers shot themselves, dreading revenge. They feared that what had happened on the Eastern front would be repeated at home. The irony was that for most Nazis, the biggest punishment turned out to be trying to resume a normal life.

After I retired—I was a hairdresser for forty years in the next town over—I decided to volunteer at Sachsenhausen. Why? It's not complicated, really. Working here reminds me that I'm alive—of little consequence, perhaps, but alive. You know why else? It gives me a reason to get dressed up every day, unlike most retirees, who let themselves go.

Even so, summer is an extremely fatiguing season. The weather changes abruptly; one day fine, the next schrecklich. Look how the sky is darkening right now. But nothing stops the tourists this time of year, not even torrential rain. Ja, they come to the camp in droves. Sometimes I get irritated answering their morbid questions, or untangling the headphones from their sweaty hair. My dear, if I still had my salon, I'd make a killing passing out coupons for my wash-and-cuts.

Stefan Hasenclever

GROßMUTTER

Stefan is the least settled in his family. That's why he lives with his grandmother in Lichtenberg. He's twenty-nine but has none of the usual markers of success: no regular job (except caring for his Oma); no steady partner (he's bisexual but leans toward men); and in every way, the opposite of his brother, a pedantic postal worker. In college, Stefan studied architecture but dropped out to travel across Tunisia. It was there he discovered his love for men. Until then Stefan had dated only dumpy hometown girls who knit him scarves for Christmas. Gemütlichkeit is no longer part of his vocabulary.

Stefan's love life has been trending toward high drama of late. He's seeing two men, on and off, as well as a married woman, whose husband works in Paris for weeks at a time. Occasionally, he sleeps with a tourist for a meal. He jokes that he's a cheap date: pea soup with bacon, bockwurst, potato salad. Basic stuff.

Occasionally, he works weekends at an antique kimono shop in Friedrichshain. The kimonos sell for a fortune to the city's elite, who have taken to wearing them as bathrobes. More and more, Stefan says, Berlin is becoming a haven for the graceless rich. This summer he's been hiring himself out as an art guide and charging sixty euros for a three-hour tour of alternative galleries. Just one of these tours keeps him eating for two weeks.

"What's the point of working if it interferes with enjoying your life?" he tells the Visitor. "It's freedom that makes you free, right?"

■

Stefan's grandmother, Wilhelmina Hasenclever, grew up in the village of Buchenwald. This summer, like every other, she works ten or more hours a day in her garden. It's the envy of the neighborhood. She grows apple trees and flowering vines, lilies, potatoes, haricots. Her roses win prizes; her plums ripen to a midnight blue. Upper arms quivering, Wilhelmina digs in the dirt with remarkable strength, moving her stool from the white asparagus to the strawberry patch, tucking loose strands of hair beneath her canvas hat. When her peonies are in bloom, their beauty is almost unbearable.

Stefan's grandmother interrupts her labors only to dispatch her daily liter of beer with Herr Toller, the long-winded butcher, who's on crutches after breaking his leg slipping on chicken fat. She and the butcher are old friends. Stefan suspects the two were sweethearts in another age, disturbing as it is for him to picture his grandmother with that bulbous-nosed dolt. Every afternoon, Herr Toller retells the same joke: how his father, a butcher before him, hung a sign in his window after the war that said: IMAGINE RAISING MEAT RATIONS NOW THAT WE'RE SO SHORT OF PAPER! Then, like clockwork, Herr Toller laughs so hard he chokes.

Oma's husband was killed in France, leaving her with two boys to raise. This she did unimaginatively, as a devout Catholic—an affliction that's become more concentrated with age. Her oldest, Stefan's father, is the "good son"—hardworking, a family man, fearful of excess. The younger one, in contrast, wore a madman's beard and died of a morphine overdose in his thirties. Stefan's parents' biggest worry is that he'll end up like his Uncle Felix. Already, rumors about Stefan are scandalizing the neighborhood: that he's a drug dealer, a pedophile, a cross-dresser—the latter stemming from his Marilyn Monroe costume for Mardi Gras last year. Stefan says the worst of the gossips is an old spinster, Ulla Gräf, who everyone knows is madly in love with Zhukov, the dead Russian general from WWII.

Recently, Stefan read in a history book that Buchenwald prisoners were sometimes hung from trees by their elbows. The locals called the excruciating result the "singing forest." In his family not a word was ever said about this singing forest, or anything else about the war, except for the same sanctioned tales of hardship: Oma's legendary three-day hunt for a lump of coal; her skill at scraping flour from the beds of flour trucks to make flour soup. These stories play like a flickering reel of horrors in the back of Stefan's brain.

His grandmother speaks very little nowadays, especially in winter, when she petrifies before the television. Her sphinx of a cat, Minka, sits beside her, slowly dying of kidney disease. On those cold lifeless days, Stefan wonders if Oma dreams of spring, of her lily bulbs detonating deep in the earth.

Yesterday, as she weeded her garden, she made Stefan promise that when her time came he would bury her in the garden under her peonies. Then she leaned toward him conspiratorially and said: "You're the only one in our entire bourgeois family who I can trust."

Yanko Petulenegro
GYPSY

Come summer, I live in the parks of Berlin. I'm no longer young but not at death's door either. I've noticed you on your morning walks around the Lietzensee, Little Sister. I don't suppose you smoke, eh? You're kind to leave me coffee on the park bench— black, the way I like it. Ah, well. I always say people need time to trust and be trusted, like animals. When I was a boy, I took care of a lot of animals: camels, horses, doves (I trained them to ride toy bicycles), and a crazy ostrich named Lala who was more trouble than the rest.

Yes, we were a traveling circus. My mother, Vioka, told fortunes while my father and sisters—Analetta, Florica, and Mala— ran the show with my uncles and cousins. The spring before the Germans came, our Lala buried her head in a hole for a fortnight and refused to show her face. Father developed itchy patches on his chest that wouldn't heal. Mama predicted that only I would survive the trouble through hard work and silence. *Silence will save you*, she told me with tears in her eyes.

I was deep in the forest collecting mandrakes for one of Mama's love potions when the Nazis found our camp. When I returned, everyone was gone, disappeared like stones dropped in a river. Little Sister, the Nazis hunted down gypsies the way they hunted down Jews. What did I do? Climbed a tree and stayed there until dawn, my stomach cramping with grief. That summer I survived on berries and the birds I felled with my slingshot. When the trees dropped their leaves, I had no place to hide and nothing more to eat. A farmer whose barn I snuck in betrayed me.

■

At Terezin, I worked in the bone-crushing mill and then in the rat-control service. The Nazis knew my worth in work, if nothing else. They flew into rages over numbers, the quotas to be filled— this many kilos of bones, that many thousands of exterminated rats, though to them rats and Jews were one and the same. Little Sister, no amount of gold could've saved the Jews in Terezin. Who you were *before* meant nothing. Let me ask you something: Have you ever seen a man beaten to death? No? Ah, then you're lucky, very lucky indeed.

After the war, everything got a lot worse before it got better. One world was ending and the other hadn't yet begun. Everyone was starving. People camped out where they could, their worldly possessions on their backs or in broken-down carts. Not so different from gypsies.

Dema Devla so me mangav. Chi mangav me barvalimo
Chi mangav me barvalimo. De man Devla zor, sastyipo . . .

My voice isn't what it used to be, Little Sister. And where is
that beautiful redheaded accordionist to accompany me? Have you
seen her at the Turkish market? Call me an orphan, if you will, but
aren't we all orphans? For where do we exist but on the margins of
history, where real lives are lived? Take a look around us. Summer
is short but inviting here—and the parks welcome a wandering
soul like me. You arrived in the spring, you say? How can you ap-
preciate the spring without living through winter?

You're here by yourself then? That's how you like it, eh? Simple,
I know. To own anything is a burden. You're a scholar, you say?
A storyteller? This doesn't surprise me. Your language gives you
away—crooked as my bad shoulder. No, it's not so much your
accent but the number of words you use. Three for every one you
need. The fewer words the better, I say.

Run away with me.
Go to hell.
Pray for me.
I love you.

What more do you need? Poetry? Poetry is in the living, Little
Sister, in the dreaming. Nobody in the world can teach you that.

IV

LAST RITES

Of these cities there will remain only what passed
through them, the wind . . .

—BERTOLT BRECHT

THE VISITOR

The train shuddered through the gritty north of Berlin before giving way to horse farms and pasturelands, church steeples and peaked roofs. Mute and immaculate—this was the German countryside. An elderly woman entered the last compartment, her face frozen on startled. Her beige shoes perfectly matched her purse. Ordinarily, the Visitor would've struck up a conversation, but today she didn't ask the woman a damn thing. She'd grown weary of history, of words.

At Sachsenhausen the Visitor learned that in the camp brothel, SS officers "tried out" the girls before allowing others use of them; that under the pretense of medical examinations, thousands of prisoners were shot with a bullet to the base of their skulls. By the killing trench, the Visitor felt short of breath. She'd read how most of Berlin's trees were cut down during the war. So much fine wood consumed by cooking stoves, or for winter warmth, or to fuel the specially rigged wood-burning cars. At the camps, guards burned corpses on train-rail grills. Women's fatty bodies burned best and so they were stacked at the base of the pyres. On cold nights the guards warmed themselves by the flames, and drank.

In the barracks, darkness gathered in the secret languages of absence. Faces etched in smoke. Facts and counterfeit truths. There was no end to the aftermath of war. "Succor," the Visitor heard whispered at the infirmary, where Nazi doctors had conducted experiments on prisoners. People asked her: "Why are you here? What do you want?" Her reasons had changed. Now it was war that kept her here; also Eros and pathos, the impossibility of looking away. A different mission.

The Visitor stopped at a Catholic church on her way back to the train station. The altar gave off a wan light. In a spotless alcove, a saint she didn't recognize was missing a wing. She lit a candle but couldn't remember a single prayer. As a child she'd gone to Catholic school and Mass, and she missed its rituals. Who besides her daughter would miss her when she was gone? Outside a brisk wind blew. Time, she thought, was her mother in hot pants and too-beige pantyhose trying to win back her wayward husband. The mother had succeeded and failed. Her husband stayed, but he continued cheating on her for the next forty years.

Recently, the Visitor heard that her mother had found evidence of yet another affair. The mother drove to the twenty-four-hour chapel on Key Biscayne and prayed to La Virgencita de la Caridad del Cobre, to whom she was devoted, to keep her from planting a fancy German cleaver in her husband's back. It didn't work. She returned home after midnight and approached him from behind (he spent most of his waking hours online). With a swift movement, she struck her husband cleanly between the shoulder blades. This stunned, but didn't kill, him. Graciously, he didn't press charges.

On the return trip to Berlin, the Visitor recited a partial list of the cities she'd visited: La Paz, Saigon, San Salvador, Kyoto, St. Petersburg, Mérida, Barcelona, Stockholm, Tokyo, Palermo, Manaus, Hue, Guatemala City, Hong Kong, Santiago, Jaipur, Port-au-Prince, Buenos Aires, Oaxaca, Montevideo, Belgrade, Lima, Naples, Havana, Quito, New Delhi, Belém . . . In all these cities, she'd lost herself, disappeared for a time, resurfaced as a new version of herself.

 That night, the Visitor dreamt of a procession of old women in a church, her mother among them. They wore loose white gowns and sang in atonal voices. The mother ambushed her in the basement. It was only the two of them in a stark white corridor. An elevator appeared in the wall and the daughter urgently pressed the call button. The mother tried to speak, but the daughter drowned her out, shouting: "The gloaming! The gloaming!" The mother receded down the corridor, as if pulled by a powerful force.

 Dreams, the Visitor thought upon waking, were the mind's invisible broom.

Volkhard W.

MIRROR

Without the mirror, he doesn't exist. He's hostage to it, spends hours gazing at himself in the faintly speckled glass, combing what's left of his hair. The baroque oval frame encircles his face, sagging with pockets of fat and displaced flesh. He's much older than he could've ever imagined becoming. As a young man, he'd denied himself nothing—women, booze, drugs—without ill effect. Now he resembles everyone else in this rundown nursing home, with their cataracts and dental plates, with their hearing aids clasped to their ears like clams.

In the 1940s, his was among the most recognizable faces of the Third Reich. Every inch the Aryan ideal, Volkhard W. played soldiers in propaganda films, paid visits to infantrymen in France and on the Eastern front (though he didn't do any fighting himself), consoled wounded civilians in hospitals. Nothing so hypnotized him as a movie camera pointed in his direction, a glimpse of his miniature face in its oversized lens. In *Eastward Wind*, his most celebrated role, he played a Great War veteran and double amputee who finds true love with a young widow in Berlin.

During the spring of 1945, an heiress named Kikka von Siewert sequestered Volkhard W. in her villa in Reinickendorf. Each time a squadron of Allied bombers droned overhead, the two scurried down to the cellar, where the hag insisted that the actor make love to her for the duration of the attack. *To die, if we must,* she said, *but in the throes of ecstasy.*

Once, Volkhard W. got caught in the capital during an air raid and fled to the Zoo Station shelter with thousands of others. Above ground, escaped chimpanzees screeched in the trees. Not a single person recognized Volkhard W. in the dark. The graffiti on the station walls told the truth: *Stalin is winning!* Outside, the antiaircraft guns thundered, and the devouring winds grew dangerous with shrapnel. When he emerged from the shelter, body parts were strewn everywhere, shriveled by fire. He forced himself to ignore the victims trapped under the smoldering debris.

After the war, the actor found work as an arsonist for failing businessmen. When asked his profession, Volkhard W. cheerfully answered: *Fireworks!* It seemed senseless to him that any citizen would deliberately destroy his property amid the devastation. As a sideline, Volkhard W. sang at funerals. His passable baritone and still-handsome face inspired the bereaved. Their most common requests: Brahms's *German Requiem: Wie lieblich sind deine Wohnungen* and Mahler's *Das Lied von der Erde*, which the actor sang with such emotion that it moistened the eyes of even the most war-hardened listeners. Occasionally, at private parties and for an extra fee, he performed the Horst Wessel Song.

Volkhard W. married four times, but the unions didn't last. By his account, his wives—Heidi, Aida, Rutilia, and Warda—simply talked too damn much. One had been lovelier than the next, but after the honeymoons, not a single one ever shut up. The more they yapped, the less desire he felt. To cope, the actor drank and gambled. And the more he drank and gambled, the louder he regretted not having fled to Hollywood when he could have. His most enjoyable days were spent as a member of the Heinrich Böll Motorcycle Club, a group of aging performance artists who took summer road trips around Germany.

After the collapse of his fourth marriage, Volkhard W. moved by himself to a ground-floor flat on Bismarckstraße. It was perfect for storing the mirrors he began amassing in the flea markets of Berlin. At its peak, his collection numbered over three hundred. Its highlights included a rare nineteenth-century French neoclassical wall mirror and a blood-red Murano in mint condition that he'd bought for a song. Most importantly, Volkhard W. was visible to himself day and night—and from every angle.

When ill health forced his move to the nursing home on Karl-Marx-Allee, only the baroque mirror with speckled glass went with him. He mourned the loss of his other mirrors and slept poorly without them. Over time, glaucoma deteriorated his vision until he could see only a tight cameo of his face. His sole friend at the nursing home, an unrepentant Nazi named Jochen Fick, fondly remembered Volkhard W.'s films, though he didn't recognize the actor himself.

On a recent overcast morning, Volkhard W. reached for his comb and gazed into the baroque mirror with speckled glass.

What looked back were not his familiar, slackening features or his red-rimmed eyelids, but a much earlier version of himself. As he watched, transfixed, the image gradually metamorphosed into a soundless, newsreel loop of his virile youth.

GEOLOGY

1.

Ricardo Soto propped one arm on his pillow and blinked into the darkness. It wasn't yet time to wake up, but there was no point in going back to sleep. He sat up and drank the tepid water on his nightstand. Slowly, he pushed himself out of bed and snapped open the shade. Across the courtyard was the former bedroom of Frau Althoff, his deceased neighbor, who'd performed fan dances for him in the eighties. "Buenos días, Mayi, buenos días, Paquito," Dr. Soto cooed as he removed the frayed towel from the lovebirds' cage.

His breakfast consisted of café con leche, cholesterol medicine, blood-pressure pills, and too many vitamins to keep straight. Dr. Soto pricked his finger to measure his blood sugar. For years, he'd smoked moderately, and though he gave it up twenty years ago—excepting an infrequent cigar—he was recently diagnosed with a choroidal melanoma. His ophthalmologist, Dr. Alves, told him that the cancer was random, that smoking had nothing to do with it. But in his experience, every pleasure in life was paid with commensurate grief.

Dr. Soto had grown up in Oriente, the easternmost province of Cuba, a place of serene mountains if not serene anything else. For all its tumultuous provincial history, the island was far from the Ring of Fire, a horseshoe-shaped string of volcanoes edging the Pacific basin. Cuba meant little to him anymore. Dr. Soto had left the island in 1963 to pursue his doctorate in East Germany and never returned, not even for the death of his father, whom he'd respected more than he'd loved.

Nearly every surface of Dr. Soto's apartment was cluttered with pyroclastic debris. In his day, he'd been a respected volcanologist. Most of what was known about ground deformation resulted directly from his research at Gunung Merapi in Indonesia. A faded photograph on the mantelpiece showed him on the Sakurajima volcano with his mentors, Katia and Maurice Krafft, who perished on Mount Unzen in 1991. Next to them was a picture of Dr. Soto's daughter, Camille, receiving her nursing school diploma in Berlin. Of her mother, Valentina Becker, or their years in Chile, there was no trace—only the black insistence of her absence.

2.

Those disastrous months after the fall of President Allende, the rise of General Pinochet—an admirer of Hitler—produced in Chile a surfeit of hysteria, paranoia, and blood-freezing fear. Valentina, who wasn't Dr. Soto's wife nor, he suspected, ever would be, was two months pregnant at the time. As dedicated as Valentina had been to her oceanographic work, she proved the opposite in love. It was Dr. Soto who'd been madly in love with her, not the other way around.

Valentina had grown up in a remote Chilean village, in the shadow of the Puyehue volcano, where days lasted an eternity and the araucaria pines howled in the winds. Her parents, as teenagers in the 1940s, had escaped Colonia Dignidad, a depraved enclave of German expatriates, where boys were sexually enslaved to its Nazi-sympathizing founder. Eventually, the colony became part of a notorious archipelago of torture centers that dotted the Chilean countryside during Pinochet's long reign.

Dr. Soto met Valentina at the University of Santiago, where she was in her second year of studies. Although the oceanography and geology departments were in the same building, Dr. Soto first spotted Valentina dancing with a folkloric troupe on a mottled quadrangle of grass. In those days, it wasn't unusual for professors to consort with their students. Everything happened so fast: her pregnancy, the birth of Camille, their brief lives together. Yet the more Dr. Soto grappled with his memories, the more unfinished their story became.

On February 2, 1972, Valentina was abducted from a bus stop in Santiago. Witnesses recalled seeing nothing out of the ordinary. (Chileans had much in common with the see-nothing Germans of World War II.) Dr. Soto often wondered what Valentina had done to get arrested, or if her abduction was simply an unfortunate collision of destiny and chance. Months later, he learned that Valentina had been wearing green, elbow-length gloves and smoking an American cigarette. Apparently, she'd come from her new lover's studio—a mediocre artist who went on to paint official portraits of Pinochet and his generals.

What did Dr. Soto have to report in the forty-one years since? Monotonous seasons as a geology professor (now emeritus) in Berlin; an amateur's devotion to birds; the intermittent joys of being father to their daughter. Camille looked enough like her mother to startle him each time they met at "their" Chinese restaurant on Kant-straße for the exact same meal: spicy shrimp and cashews for her; wonton soup and moo shu pork for him.

Dr. Soto never married—much too gloomy, his former lovers complained—though he once fell for a crippled German ballerina who'd danced in Havana in the fifties. As usual, their affair was brief and ended badly. His own daughter was childless, with two failed marriages behind her. Creatures of habit, he and Camille lived separately in their solitudes, their birdsong (they kept parrots, lovebirds, and African parakeets between them), and their inability to sustain a long-term interest in others. The two were never so compatible as when they were melancholic together. It was as if Valentina's absence continued to exert on them an unrelenting, placental hold. This was their curse, their morbid loyalty to her.

3.

Valentina was neither spontaneous nor extravagant, yet people often remembered her as such. In fact, she'd meted out her energies precisely. If, for example, she decided that baby Camille was crying for no discernible reason, Valentina ignored her without a shred of guilt. She had many fine qualities, but a maternal instinct wasn't one of them. It was Dr. Soto who'd fed Camille, changed her diapers, entertained her with silly faces and songs. And, at Valentina's insistence, he agreed to have another child with her.

"The biological imperative," Dr. Soto told the Visitor, "is stronger than any sensible man's ability to evade it."

When Valentina disappeared, Chileans of her generation had enjoyed the luxury of democracy—a flawed democracy, but democracy nonetheless. When the Revolution had swept to power in Cuba, the euphoria was short-lived. Thugs and innocents alike were dragged to the firing squads without trials or due process. Dr. Soto's father's leather factory was confiscated, and he was forced to attend the ceremony transferring CUEROS DE SOTO to the state. What most galled the elder Soto were the shoddy belts and handbags produced under the new "management." On the day he whitewashed his name off the factory sign, he was put under house arrest.

As a Cuban national, Dr. Soto was at a disadvantage working in Pinochet's Chile. Castro was blamed for everything in those days: exporting Communism, brainwashing students, the collapse of Chile's faltering economy. At one point, Dr. Soto was briefly jailed for attacking a precinct captain who'd called Valentina a whore. Dr. Soto assumed that she'd been murdered, but how could he prove it? Nobody could prove anything in those days and live to tell about it. Seven months after her abduction, Dr. Soto fled with their daughter to East Berlin. He accepted a teaching position at Humboldt University, his alma mater.

That first winter in the divided city was bleak. The temperature regularly dropped below zero, and the endless gray of the skies depressed Dr. Soto to the bone. He and Camille lived in a cramped fourth-floor walk-up near the Staatsoper. Their back window overlooked a mature chestnut tree, desolate in winter but alive with nightingales in the spring.

In what spare time he had, Dr. Soto circulated petitions against Pinochet's mounting abuses, underscoring the dictator's connections to the Nazis. Camille reached the expected milestones without fanfare. The years flew by until one day Dr. Soto failed to recognize himself in a tram window. Youth had turned its back on him forever.

4.

This afternoon, Dr. Soto received more bad news from his ophthalmologist. His cancer, Dr. Alves said, was spreading. It was unclear to him now what the future held except a more precipitous end. She recommended that he see an ophthalmic oncologist before it was too late.

"Too late for what?" he retorted, bristling.

"To save your life."

"So, you think I'm afraid of dying?"

Physicians, he knew, were myopically trained to prolong life. Never mind what the body decreed. If it weren't for his daughter,

Dr. Soto might have ended his life long ago. After leaving Dr. Alves's office, he walked along the Spree River to empty his mind. On weekends, he often enjoyed watching the tango dancers on its banks. The river's glistening surface reminded him of sliding plate glass. Gulls soared above him, swiveling on gusts of wind.

On his way home, Dr. Soto stopped at the tobacconist's and splurged on two Cohiba Espléndidos. He offered one to the Visitor, though he was ambivalent about her interest in him.

"Please take one," Dr. Soto insisted, against her protests. "May it bring you closer to what you seek in Berlin."

SIGNALS

A scent accompanies her,
less a scent
than a sweet pressure of the air
against my brain . . .

—GOTTFRIED BENN

Dead moths litter the windowsill of Raya's hospital room. When she takes a deep breath—like that, see?—her eyes flutter as if they might reopen. Every hour or so, I wipe the crust of dried tears from her lashes with a damp handkerchief. Sixty-eight years ago, Berlin fell to us. I say "us," Dear Visitor, because we were with the victors. Raya Semenovna and I were signalers then, sticking together during the campaign west. The brutal months of winter fighting finally yielded to the muddy relief of spring. In the push toward Berlin, we helped control the roads into the city, blazed night into day with our searchlights.

My grief as Raya's death grows near is more than I can bear. When we met, she was a strong village girl who could drop off to sleep in a snowstorm. And she could match, drink for drink, any soldier in our battalion. Now I fear that Raya won't ever wake up again. On Thursday she suffered a cerebral hemorrhage and slipped into a coma. Her heart remains strong, but her mind is unlikely to recover. Our son, Osip Pyotrovich, is rushing here from Kazakhstan, where he's a petrochemical engineer.

Our story is long but if it pleases you, I can offer you a few details. On the march to Berlin, Raya got pregnant. A stray bullet killed the father, Pyotr Ivanovich Kurpatov, the very morning after their tryst. Raya didn't cry at the news—not then, or ever. She hid the pregnancy under her Red Army coat. Only I knew the truth. As the Shturmoviks flew overhead, Raya and I swore that when the war ended, we'd return home and raise our children together (she encouraged me to get pregnant, too). Our plan? To tell everyone that our husbands had died at the front. Who could dispute us?

Try the postal clerk, Raya said, prodding me. *He's a gentle one.* And so I waited at the end of a long line of soldiers who were sending their loot home.

"Germans smashed my house. Take it! If you don't, you're not the post office!" the harelipped sniper shouted, thrusting forward panes of glass he'd tied together with wire.

Other soldiers sent home sacks of nails or Gretchen knickers. I laughed, imagining how their wives would react.

Our best gunner handed over a rolled-up saw.

"You could've wrapped it, at least," the postal clerk snarled. This was Anatoly Borisovich, the fellow Raya had recommended.

"I've just come from the front!" the gunner huffed. He wore a pilfered pink brassiere as earmuffs.

"And where's the address?" Anatoly Borisovich demanded.

"On the saw. Here, see?" He pointed to the faint scratching on the blade.

Finally, Anatoly Borisovich shrugged and accepted the package. Two more men stepped up with their booty crudely sewn in sheets. They'd paid an old Frau in fresh bread for this handiwork. Another showed up with a box of light bulbs, each carefully wrapped in a scrap of felt. By the time it was my turn, Anatoly Borisovich glared at me, exasperated.

"What do you want?" he barked.

I looked behind me before leaning toward him and whispered: "To find comfort in your arms."

It was true that Anatoly Borisovich was a gentle lover, but he didn't impregnate me. *You're too thin*, Raya scolded. *You have to fatten yourself up.* Russian men, then as now, prefer plump partridges, rolls of buttery flesh to hold and squeeze. I was an unappealing sack of bones. No doubt my distaste for men's coarseness dampened my enthusiasm.

■

When the time came to storm the Führer's bunker, Raya and I were selected to accompany the elite troops. This was a great honor. The bunker looked as if Hitler had been expecting guests—the kitchen well stocked, the cutlery arranged, fresh jonquils on the dining table. But on the roof, pyres of ash still smoked. Those Nazi cowards had killed themselves rather than face the Russian music. Worst of all, we found six dead children inside, the oldest with bruises on her face. Later, we learned that they were Goebbel's kids and their mother had force-fed them cyanide.

Raya and I were assigned to comb through Eva Braun's quarters. Such luxuries we found! Raya took great delight in tickling me with an ostrich plume plucked from a blue satin hat. Then she sprayed me with so much perfume I doubled over coughing, my eyes watering.

"Look at this!" Raya squealed, throwing me a silver fox fur cape. I took it to please her, but it was she who wore it after the war.

She tried on a sparkling white evening gown embroidered with crystals. After months of army uniforms, the sight of Raya's radiant breasts (swollen from her pregnancy) shocked us both. Embarrassed, I busied myself trying on Eva's shoes—our feet were exactly the same size—but took nothing for myself.

■

Dear Visitor, this Spanish talcum powder is Raya's favorite. She used to dust it on herself after every bath. Here, take a whiff. It's a blend of sandalwood and roses. Poor Raya doesn't smell like herself anymore, and her hair has a faint carbolic scent. After the Wall fell, Raya practically led the mob that stampeded on KaDeWe, the luxury department store on the Ku'damm. She couldn't get enough of Western face creams, bubble baths, nail polish, eye shadows. Ah, my Raya was feminine to her core. How could I resent the expense? To see her happy made me happy. I had no other goal in life.

After I visit Raya, I go to the cemetery nearby. It's dedicated to the Russian soldiers who died in the battle for Berlin. I remember our friends—Daniil Karpovich Fedorenko, Vasily Sergeyevich Leptev, Stepan Stepanovich Gushin, Elena Glebovna Artyomov, a signaler like us, who died with six others in a direct tank hit. Elena had loved wristwatches and wore a dozen up and down her arms. All the soldiers were obsessed with them. Most of us had at least three—one set to Moscow time, one to Berlin, and another to our hometowns.

Have you seen that famous photo of Russian soldiers raising our flag on the Reichstag? Did you know that it had to be officially altered? That's right. Too many stolen watches on the conquerors' arms!

After the fall of Berlin, our platoon was lucky to get a requisitioned house in what must've once been a rich district. Even badly damaged, the place was beautiful: a bathtub big enough for two, a walk-in freezer, ceilings high enough to stack three Russian huts. Why had Hitler attacked us when his own people lived so much better than ours? In the library, we found a parrot squawking "Heil Hitler!" next to a bronze bust of the Führer. The damn bird wouldn't shut up, so we shot it full of holes. As for Hitler's bust, we dug a pit in the garden, dropped the bronze to the bottom, and used it as a latrine.

Victory wasn't the end of our suffering, Dear Visitor. Thousands of Red Army veterans were deported to the gulag on false charges of collaborating with the enemy. Every last soldier understood that it was better to die fighting than to be taken prisoner. Stalin's own son, who'd died a POW, was a source of deep shame to his father. Imagine battling so long and so hard, surviving a Nazi death camp—Russian soldiers were starved without mercy—only to be charged as a traitor to the Motherland? (And the "samovars," the limbless ones, were treated worst of all!) There are no words for such disgrace.

Raya and I were very fortunate. With my high school German, I served as a "tongue" for our local commander. Each morning I sat by his side, translating Berliners' complaints about food shortages, collapsing buildings, the lack of medical care, rapes, suicides, the rotting corpses everywhere. The commander settled every squabble—a thousand things you wouldn't think of. Raya carried on directing traffic in the mess of the streets. Here's a photo of her with her batons after the war.

Yes, she was very beautiful. This was taken before the commander, at my insistence, hired her as caretaker for his growing menagerie: peacocks, dachshunds, breeder goats, a French-speaking cockatiel, and a prizewinning dairy cow named Thilde. Because our commander was a country boy at heart, our headquarters became a farmyard.

Despite the difficulties—the ruins, the refugees—I look back on those days with a fond nostalgia. After Berlin was divided, Raya and I continued on in the East (she in a bottle factory; me as a language teacher) and quietly raised our son. Few people at the time would've believed we had a right to our happiness, and yet somehow, miraculously, we attained it. As time went on and our dear Osip grew into a fine young man, Raya and I joked that we had the best "marriage" of anyone we knew.

Dear Visitor, the heart is immeasurable. Infinitely so. But I fear that Raya may have already passed to the shadows. What's left for me now but to hope for one last miracle?

Ernst Feuchtwanger

PUNK

There's a photograph of me at the old Stasi headquarters in Lichtenberg. I heard that they'd turned the place into a fucking museum, and I wanted to have a look. Back in the day, Liebchen, I was known as Roto, punk bassist for DEINE MUTTER!, the most notorious East German band of the seventies. That asshole of a tour guide said our band members were all Stasi agents. Wrong! Only three of the five of us were. Then he quoted a music critic who'd once described me as *talentless as a surly bear*. The tourists laughed when he said it, too, like it was the most fucking hilarious thing they'd ever heard. I had half a mind to stop them in their tracks and yell: *We did our patriotic duty and now you have the nerve to ridicule us?*

I was thirty-five when that picture was taken, though I looked a lot younger. I had a nice head of hair then, enough for a Mohawk. The piercings hurt like hell, I'm not gonna lie—and they got fucking infected all the time—but the girls loved 'em. Nee, I wouldn't call myself a musician. Three or four chords were all it took. The rest was attitude. Liebchen, what do you *think* I was doing? Spying on the underground. Protecting our country from destabilizing elements. My biggest strength was recognizing people's weaknesses. Still is. I can look at you right now—mousy, not one for the limelight, sensitive antennae—and know you trust nobody. Who stole from you? Your daddy? I knew it. I told you I was good. Shrinks got nothing on me.

Sicher, I locked away my share of delinquents. No spook rings or anything like that, but I did a good job. Enough to get me promoted to the number two position in the Degenerate Artists Unit. What?! I'm gonna ignore that remark since you're not from around here. Listen up. We targeted subversives, saved the country time and again, exploited political hostilities to our advantage. Those were our glory days, Liebchen. And it all came crashing down with the Berlin Wall. Communism abandoned *us*. That's right, we Stasi were loyal to the bitter end—on high alert, waiting for the order to crack heads, to do whatever was necessary. But the order never came. They sold us out big time. Big. Time.

Fortunately, I managed to destroy my files, then slipped over to the West and started a new life. Most agents weren't so lucky. I know ex-Stasi who are living on the streets of Berlin. Drinking, mostly. They couldn't adapt. The world we knew was flipped over like a fucking fried egg. You know, there was a time when nobody could touch us. Not the KGB. Not the Gestapo. Not even SAVAK.

And we didn't have the, eh, *publicity* those organizations had. That's part of what made us so great. Even your hotshot Castro came to us for advice.

Liebchen, if I sound proud, it's because I *am* proud. We had our bad apples, like anywhere else. Hey, corporations have a helleva lot more psychopaths than we ever did. When you were inside the Stasi, the way I was for twenty-three years, you were a made man. For someone of humble origins like me, you couldn't go any higher. My father had been a train porter his whole life. A month after he retired, he dropped dead taking a nap in the garden. Mutti swears it's because he stopped moving.

After the shitstorm, I began selling fancy eye equipment to hospitals in the West. I started off with Swiss slit lamps and operating microscopes, then moved on to optical coherence tomography machines at sixty thousand euros a pop. Hell, yeah. You better believe I'm a quick study. My commissions got *this* fat in no time. I was living the high life, all-out bourgeois—ha! Nee, I don't play bass anymore. A few of the old songs still run through my head, though: "Sigfrieda Is a Punk Rocker," "The KGB Took My Baby Away." Acknowledged, Liebchen, acknowledged. I never said we were the most original band on the planet. The Ramones were *everyone's* gods in those days, not just yours. What the fuck? No way I'm gonna sing for you, or anyone else. Who the hell would've bought medical equipment from me if they'd known I was the badass formerly known as Roto?

Friends? Not too many left. Never married either, though there's someone I see on a regular basis. She isn't my Freundin exactly, but we get together on weekends for an hour or two and have a fine-enough time. That's all I'm gonna tell you, goddamit. I'm not one of those guys who looks back on his life with a shitload of regrets. My blood pressure's on the high side and my kidney stones act up now and then, but that's about it. Like I said, I'm living an easy retirement. Liebchen, how many ex-Stasi punk rockers do you know who can say that?

Ulla Gräf

ZHUKOV (SECRET) ADMIRATION
SOCIETY FOR LADIES

So, you've found me. You're certainly persistent, I'll grant you that. Bitte, forgive my reluctance, but the subject is a sensitive one. It's true that I'm president of the Zhukov (Secret) Admiration Society for Ladies. Ja, I'm the last member since Hedy passed away four years ago. She and I used to go regularly to the German-Russian Museum in Karlshorst to view the film clip we knew by heart: that of Germany's unconditional military surrender to Marshal Georgy Konstantinovich Zhukov on May 8, 1945.

Ah, that was the commander's finest hour! To understand Berlin, the war, everything, you absolutely must see it. Dear Georgy betrays no emotion in this extraordinary footage, behaving with the dignity that befits a man of his stature—the brilliant Russian strategist who never lost a battle. *We invite the German delegation to sign the act of capitulation.* Sicher. He was the opposite of the Reich's repellant, arrogant, *doomed* leaders. Why, those criminals had the hubris to balk even at the moment of surrender! Afterward my Georgy danced the russkaya until dawn with his cheering generals.

Selbstverständlich, my admiration for him is boundless. This is beside the point, but don't you agree that Georgy was an exceptionally handsome man in his prime? The dimple in his chin, his clear-eyed gaze, the keen intelligence in his bearing—a peasant intelligence refined by experience and honor. To think that as a youth, he'd been apprenticed to a furrier in Moscow! Lucky for history, he was conscripted into the Red Army, launching a career that entranced me as a schoolgirl, despite the vicious propaganda against him. Kind Visitor, I refused two marriage proposals as a young woman—and that was when men were scarce. Nobody, nobody could ever compete with my Georgy.

You must understand that I still take great pains to conceal my devotion, especially with my neighbors. For how could I publicly admit to loving the man who broke the back of the Wehrmacht, who killed our fathers and grandfathers, whose soldiers violated our mothers? Impossible. Personally, I don't believe that the excesses of his troops should taint Georgy himself. What I consider most important is the man's genius, his raw energy, the taste of his name on my tongue. Such an affliction I suffer!

Hedy went so far as to suggest that Georgy might very well have been my father. It isn't as far-fetched as it sounds, Kind Visitor. Unsurprisingly, Georgy was something of a ladies' man. He's known to have sired three daughters with three different women—and there were rumors of several more. Why couldn't I have been one of them? Take a good look at my face. Closer. Don't you see how Georgy lives on in my gaze, in my bearing? In truth, the identity of my biological father remains a mystery. After the war, Mutti tried to cover this up by marrying a sullen Finnish sailor who formally adopted me.

My favorite story about Georgy? There are countless. How could I possibly choose? Ah, well, there was that time Stalin was thrown from his Arabian stallion and angrily decreed: "Let Zhukov take the parade!" Meaning the victory parade. He fully expected that Georgy, too, would be thrown from the horse and publicly humiliated. But on a tip from Stalin's younger son, Georgy spent days mastering the stallion. As the band played "Glory to You!" thousands of veterans marched in the rain to Red Square and hurled the Nazi banner at Stalin's feet. Georgy, magnificent as ever, rode Stalin's horse without incident to the roar of the adoring crowd.

You are sympathetic, Kind Visitor, I can see that. You're not apt to judge me, as my countrymen might. It wasn't your war, after all. Why don't you join me at Karlshorst on Tuesday? Then you can see for yourself what I'm talking about. The photographs of Georgy are quite dashing. He was a giant of a man with a broad chest, but never broad enough for all his medals. Every winter I celebrate his birthday by baking sturgeon kulebyaka pies. And in June, I commemorate Georgy's death by raising a glass or two to his memory. How is it possible that he's been gone from us these thirty-nine long years?

Bitte, I beseech you: don't go around telling anyone about me. I'm much too old to suffer reprisals. Ach du meine Güte, I hope I'm not making a mistake confiding in you . . .

Rodrigo Mejía
BONGOS

Fifteen years ago, my goal was simple: to get the hell out of Cuba. It was the Special Period, and everyone was totally broke. The sure-fire way off the island was to marry a tourist. Planeloads of them arrived in Havana every day. My compays zeroed in on the desperate middle-aged chicks. A lot of them were divorced and rich enough, at least, to take a Caribbean vacation. Bueno, after a little island-style seducing and bureaucratic rigmarole, the luckiest of my friends took off for Sweden, Spain, Canada, even the U.S. If you were a musician, like me, a bongosero, and halfway presentable, this wasn't impossible.

Fredi Milanés, the best timbalero in Old Havana, married a cincuentona from the French Riviera. When they split up a year later, he got a big cash settlement and became a blackjack dealer in Monaco. That bastard pulls in a fortune every night! The worst off of us is Pepito Alarcón, a phenomenal trumpeter. He ended up in Miami con una loca named Gladys. She'd already been divorced four times and wasn't about to agree to a fifth, so she made Pepito's life a pure misery. El pobre infeliz has been reduced to playing his trumpet for spare change outside the Versailles in Little Havana.

Gerta was forty-two when we met in Old Havana. She got pregnant immediately—with twin boys; I don't mess around! This sped up my visa application. My wife isn't exactly what you'd call a great beauty. She's six feet tall and outweighs me by sixty pounds. Still, she was better than a lot of the old bats who flocked to Cuba. I could've done a lot worse is what I'm telling you. But the shit's crazy here, corazón. Gerta's family flipped out when their only daughter—a fancy divorce lawyer—married poor humble me. You know what they told her? *Keep the babies and run!* They call me "the Negro" and "the Mexican" to my face. Comemierdas. But what's the use of my cursing out people who don't understand a word I'm saying?

Mira, I survived the fucking Revolution, and I'll survive this, too. I speak Spanish with my sons, but I can feel it evaporating, stranding me between two cultures, two languages. And it's not just any Spanish, but *Cuban* Spanish. Who else knows what it means to *comer un cable?* You can say someone's fucked over, but it's just not the same thing. Or how do you translate that *fulano de tal no tiene dos dedos de frente?* It means the guy is stupid, sure, but who the hell else calls it "not having two fingers of forehead"? That's right, like a Neanderthal. See, I've got you laughing already!

What hurts the most is that my sons are learning more about becoming men from their mother than from me. In Havana we might stand around all day arguing sports, but officially, at least, we had jobs. Gerta doesn't get this. Equality, equality, she says. But it's not all about equality between men and women! Where's the dance, the push and pull of flirtation? This is high art in Cuba; I don't have to tell you. That's one thing the Revolution couldn't take away from us. On Sundays, Gerta drops off the boys at her parents' apartment and returns home to make love to me. Fifteen minutes is all it takes. Then we fix lunch and watch the news, like a couple of mannequins. Sí, muy triste.

You don't know how good it feels to connect with you, corazón. It's not easy to transplant, to rearrange my roots so radically. Sometimes I dream of returning to Havana, but I'm not a complete idiot. Why should I trade back one prison for another? Besides, nobody's left for me there anymore. My compays are gone and my parents died six years ago—así, one after the other. Maybe I'll leave Berlin when my boys are grown. By then Cuba will be different, the old guard dead. I don't care what anyone says; until the Castros are six feet under, nothing's going to change.

What? Can you see me trying to divorce a divorce lawyer? Not to mention that Gerta is the best in Berlin. She'd cut my balls off without blinking. Eso mismo. She stays calm, nothing ruffles her, and then when you least expect it, she snaps you in two like a caimán.

Perdóname, corazón, but I have to pick up my sons from school. Detlev has a fencing lesson, and Lutz needs to go to his math tutor. Encantado de conocerte. Perhaps you'd like to go dancing sometime? ¿A mí con ese cuento? There's no such thing as a cubana who can't dance! I know a place in Mitte, a converted beer factory that has live salsa on Wednesday nights. ¿Que dices?

La Roswitha

LAST KAFFEE

You ask me if I would do it again? Jump off the truck evacuating us from Normandy? Ah, but that first sip of coffee was pure ambrosia, darling, pure ambrosia. How else could I have faced another jolting ride in that Wehrmacht jeep? My sweet Oskar, afraid that he'd be left behind, ignored my request for coffee and warned me against fetching it myself. Why, of course I forgave him. For in the very instant that missile hit, all was ecstasy! This surprises you? What would you rather have me say? Darling, our fates are quite precise. I've reached a state of bliss. There's no future where I am, only a fully, deliciously endless now.

■

On her last morning alive, Roswitha wore a lavender corset under her sequined gown, which was also lavender and embroidered with lilacs. Though she had the stature of a nine-year-old, she lacked nothing of a grown woman's attributes. To her admirers, Roswitha was all the more delectable for her proportions. A rare truffle, they agreed—bewitching, sublime. She specialized in introducing young men to the delights of the flesh. A new lover had to be trained, not tamed, his enthusiasms harnessed to please, please, please. How she'd enjoyed leaving her signature teeth marks around their nipples and knees. Oskar Matzerath would forever remember his affair with Roswitha as the happiest of his life.

Despite the panicked exodus from Normandy, Roswitha's luggage had been neatly stacked in the jeep. Her lashes were curled, her cheeks smoothed with age-defying potions and a hint of rouge. On her feet were a pair of minuscule feathered mules. Roswitha was partial to kitten heels, and she'd worn these, her favorite, throughout the Eastern front, where soldiers carried her like a pint-size queen above the mud and carnage.

■

I used to unfold an ornate portable mirror and invite my lovers to gaze at themselves, handsomely naked beside me. We must be pleasing to ourselves before we can please others, n'est-ce-pas? Call me ritualistic, darling, but in the boudoir, I was anything but predictable. Nothing of significance can be expressed without the body. To praise and be praised; for this we were created. Illusion is the daily bread of artists—we live for illusion, cry for illusion—all the while remaining conscious of time's slippage. For we know too well that mortality can strike from one moment to the next, like Churchill's missile. In the end, it's all theater. And I felt nothing but a blinding astonishment. Can you imagine a better exit?

■

Her name was Roswitha, and her life was dedicated to the immediacy of wonder, and to pleasure. For her there was no second act, only perpetual surrender. Why else would she have ignored Oskar's warnings (and those of the lovesick Wehrmacht captain) and dashed for that last cup of coffee? Why else but to light up the skies with her spangled flesh?

Lukas Böhm

TUXEDO

Every morning begins the same way: with the dull thud of a bird hitting a window of my high-rise apartment in Mitte. Turkish coffee in hand—a habit I acquired in the sixties—I await the sudden death of yet another wayward sparrow (they're mostly sparrows). What do I have to look forward to today? Only an appointment with my eye doctor, a statuesque African woman who, except for her advancing pregnancy, looks to me like a wondrously handsome man. Dr. Alves will warn me again that my cataracts are hardening, that without an operation I'll likely lose my vision.

Already my eyes have the luster of the mother-of-pearl buttons on my old dress shirts, which hang in the closet alongside my tuxedos. The next time I wear a tuxedo, Dear Visitor, will be at my funeral. I've specified this in my will. And I'm to be buried with my A clarinet, a vintage Buffet I inherited from my father. Decades ago, he was the much-heralded principal clarinetist of the Berlin Philharmonic (the youngest in its history). He took his own life as the Russians stormed Berlin. I was just thirteen then and had been playing the clarinet for five years but never, my father admonished me, with sufficient fervor.

Attired in his spotless concert dress, Father hanged himself with a length of knotted silk cravats, which he'd fastened to our half-shattered chandelier. It was I who found him in the shambles of our music room. The bombs had fallen with metronomic regularity for months, but, thankfully, we'd been spared a direct hit. Our flat was on the outskirts of Berlin and only moderately damaged—walls cracked, the plaster fallen. I can still recall the din of the air raids that so flattened the city. Without the smoke, we could see for fifty miles in every direction. Father's neck was bruised a deep mauve—a color I've since detected only in rare tropical orchids. In that moment, I understood that my life was no longer my own.

The previous winter, my mother and I had grown alarmed at Father's escalating histrionics, his fits of melancholy, the dramatic gestures she ascribed to the temperament he'd inherited from his Galician grandmother, who'd run off with a common garrison soldier during the Spanish-American War. Some days Father would lie in bed, inert and speechless; on others, he maniacally repaired the cracks in the walls with candle wax and curses. His nerves worsened after he listened to foreign radio reports, a highly illegal pastime. I believe now that he was searching for a reason to live. When I discovered his body, Mother was off in the countryside with my brother, Herbert—not quite two at the time—bartering our silverware for root vegetables.

Dear Visitor, it's crucial to understand that the Philharmonic was the cultural crown jewel of the Third Reich. Its conductor then, Wilhelm Furtwängler, did everything in his power to protect his Jewish musicians. The orchestra revered him, my father included. Furtwängler declined numerous offers to immigrate, including the directorship of the Chicago Symphony. Instead he chose to remain with the German people in their darkest hour. For how could he have left our music—the music of Brahms, and Beethoven, and Mahler—in the hands of the Nazis? When bombs destroyed his concert hall, Furtwängler proceeded to conduct at the Staatsoper and then at the Admiralspalast. My father noted the final program in his diary: "Die Zauberflote ov., Mozart Symph. no. 40 (1st 2 mvmts), & Brahms 1st."

In his suicide note, Father blamed the emotional strain of performing Bruckner's Symphony no. 7 in E Major as the bombs fell on Berlin. He fretted over Russia and its genius composers— Shostakovich was a forbidden favorite. Father was terrified of a Soviet invasion and the vague, subjugated future that awaited us under Bolshevism. Nonetheless, he was imperiously specific regarding my musical education: how often I was to practice and perform; where and with whom I should study (with Torsten Niederberger in Vienna when I turned fifteen); and the precise order of pieces I was to master, culminating, surprisingly, with Nielsen's contemporary masterwork, Clarinet Concerto, op. 57.

Dear Visitor, how can I convey to you the extent of Germany's ruin? From the delusional heights of the so-called master race, we were reduced to living like rats in the rubble. Our once great capital had become a veritable necropolis. To this day, I suffer night terrors, flinch at the clap of lightning or an unexpected clash of cymbals. After the war, nobody dared complain about the devastation either. Was our shame so great that it silenced us? Or was our resistance to shame the greater silencer?

My mother, a resourceful woman, was fluent in English and French. This served her well in our post-apocalyptic world. With help from Father's music connections, she shipped me off to study in Vienna. She and Herbert moved to Paris—a miracle in itself—and eventually opened what became the finest lingerie shop in the city. The pent-up demand for luxury goods and the quality of her inventory soon made her a very wealthy woman. Little Herbert grew up without the privations that had plagued my childhood. For him, our father's absence was mitigated by Mother's remarriage to a childless widower, a kindly bicycle manufacturer of stable means.

Thanks to Father's careful instructions, my tone and technique grew flawless (please permit me this immodesty). He'd often said that music was the principal tonic for the disorders of civilization, that nothing could be expressed without it. But for me, it became the grammar of submission. In due course, I took his place as the *second* youngest clarinetist ever appointed to the Berlin Philharmonic. The other musicians welcomed me warmly on my first day—tapping their bows, shuffling their feet—in homage to my legendary father. And there I remained for the duration of my career.

On my fiftieth anniversary with the orchestra, the city's musical elite threw me a grand party, and, regrettably, the ancient business about Father was dredged up. A crone with unblinking eyes and sporting a cherry-red bowler (I'd never met her before, or seen her since) disclosed that she'd known him in her youth, intimating that she and my father had been lovers during the war. All I could think to say, before turning on my heels, was: *You stupid, stupid woman!* I repented my hastiness. For who knew what she might've revealed to me about him?

No sooner were the anniversary festivities over than our conductor persuaded me to retire. In truth, he was attempting to make room for a young clarinetist (also a product of the Niederberger dynasty) for whom many notable orchestras were vying. His movie-star looks are plastered on posters all over Berlin. Haven't you seen them? Dark hair, smug expression, eyes deliberately smoldering. In one of his shameless promotional videos, he traipses around the city ogling women and wielding his clarinet like a priapic baton. Yes, Dear Visitor, it is quite unseemly.

My apartment faces east, and the view is perpetually congested with gargantuan red and yellow cranes. Those of us in the West persist, as we have for twenty-three years, in bringing East Berlin into the twenty-first century. This effort, I'm afraid, has wholly bankrupted our city. (Personally, I could live without the monumentally oppressive Alexanderplatz.) Yet I understand very well the resistance to change, the longing for stasis and familiarity. Now I, too, am collapsing from age and neglect. My eyes are clouded, my hands no longer steady. And I wait for death, without Father's courage, to end it on my own terms.

Dear Visitor, upward of two hundred sparrows a year die against my windows, blinded by what they can't see.

EPILOGUE

It was August, and the Visitor's time in Berlin was nearing an end.

She bought a cheap point-and-shoot and began taking photographs, longing for a higher incidence of happy accident. She'd come to Berlin for stories, and the city had been more than generous. Mostly, she'd listened. There was, she knew, poetry in the listening. She didn't belong here, but there was room for her. Maybe that was enough.

Her daughter came for the Visitor's last weeks in Berlin. Summer was in its full glory, the twilights prolonged, the parks alive with music. They lingered in the city's flea markets and coffee shops, ate Russian borscht, attended fashion shows and concerts, rode bikes in the Tiergarten, watched movies under the stars. They went to the aquarium and studied the puffer fish and a "false map" turtle sunning itself on a rock. One evening, her daughter jokingly gave her a check for a million dollars. In the subject line was a small, hand-drawn heart.

In a taxi on their way to the airport, the Visitor received word that her mother had died swimming in Key Biscayne Bay. It wasn't indifference she felt, but a sad wonderment. The mother was dead, and yet she was still alive. How was that possible? Here in Berlin, the Visitor had listened to others' histories and was finally released from her own. And now? What did she want? Quiet, resplendent days in the light. Her daughter a breath away. And a butterfly net with which to swipe the air, trapping bits of flying color here and there. Yes, she might spend the rest of her life doing nothing more than that.

DAS ENDE

ACKNOWLEDGMENTS

Mil gracias to Alfredo Franco, who encouraged me to spend time in Berlin, regaled me with irresistible stories, and read this novel over and again with insight and generosity. A shout-out to Scott Brown, whom I've had the privilege to know for over half my life and whose friendship and editorial acuity I value ever more with the years. Deep gratitude to Dan Smetanka, my editor at Counterpoint Press, whose eye is unfailing—and from whom I simply couldn't ask for more. And to Ellen Levine, dear friend and literary agent extraordinaire, who worked tirelessly to find this book its rightful home.

I had the great pleasure of meeting Werner Sollors and benefited enormously from his tales and his extraordinary book *The Temptation of Despair.* Timothy Snyder's monumental *Bloodlands:*

Europe Between Hitler and Stalin opened the floodgates of a complex, tragic history that informs these pages, as did Antony Beevor's *The Fall of Berlin 1945*, W. G. Sebald's *On the Natural History of Destruction*, and Wendy Lower's *Hitler's Furies: German Women in the Nazi Killing Fields*, among other titles.

Besitos to my daughter, Pilar García-Brown, fellow traveler and avid reader, who spent five weeks with me in Berlin, kindly read this book, and offered excellent suggestions. Lastly, to my husband, Gary Aguilar, who sustains me, heart and soul, every single day.

CRISTINA GARCÍA is the author of seven novels, including *Dreaming in Cuban*—a finalist for the National Book Award—*The Agüero Sisters*, *Monkey Hunting*, *A Handbook to Luck*, *The Lady Matador's Hotel*, and *King of Cuba*. Her work has been translated into fourteen languages. García has edited anthologies, written children's books, published poetry, and taught at universities nationwide. She lives in the San Francisco Bay area. Learn more at www.cristinagarcianovelist.com.